Forbidden Gorge

Forbidden Gorge

And Other Tales

C. N. Nageswara Rao

PARTRIDGE

To order additional copies of this book, contact
Partridge India
000 800 10062 62
orders.india@partridgepublishing.com

www.partridgepublishing.com/india

CONTENTS

Dedicated to

My Father-in-Law Buddha Ramachandra Rao,
Executive Engineer (Retd), Nagarjuna Sagar Dam
and Mother-in-Law Buddha Ramanamma

ACKNOWLEDGEMENT

If I have written this book, it is because of great support and encouragement that I have received from my friends, colleagues, teachers, bosses, well wishers and family members. I wish to express my sincere thanks to one and all of them.

I express my sincere thanks to Sri Tenneti Sudhakar Rao, former Executive Director (HR), Wg. Cdr. R. K. Chawla (Retd), Sri Tangirala Rammohan and other friends, who gave their invaluable opinion on my first book. I sincerely thank Sri V. Srinivasan, former Executive Director (Avionics Division), Sri M. Sita Raman, Sri Chinta Rajeswara Rao, Sri B. Radhakishan, Sri S. R. Suresh, Sri Dasaratha Atma, Sri M. Padmakar Rao, Sri Ramachandra Diwakar, Sri R. G. Bansod, Sri R. Sivaraj, Sri K. S. N. Reddy, Sri D. V. Latkar, Sri Nazimuddin, Sri Pingali Sundara Rama Rao, Sri Subas Chand and Sri Janmeday Das from Hindustan Aeronautics Limited. I also express my thanks to Sri S. Madhava Rao from Hyderabad Allwyn and Sri Ghosh from National Geophysical Research Institute.

I thank my former colleagues Sri S. V. Sastry, Sri B. N. Sudarshan, Sri P. Ramachandriah, Sri A. Dharma Rao, Sri A. Gangadhara Rao, Sri K. V. Reddy, Sri M. Srinivasulu, Sri G. Venkatesham, Sri M. Jitendernath Thakur, Sri K. Nagi Reddy, Sri V. C. Rami Reddy, Sri Viyyanna, Sri Vadrevu Ramaseshagiri Rao, Sri V. Ramakrishna rao, Sri P. Narasing Rao, Sri K. C. Sasidhara, Sri N. Sameer, Sri V. Madhusudana Reddy and other associates.

I would like to express my sincere thanks to Sri Marepally Sammi Reddy, Capt. Reddy (Retd) and Sri Chitukula Narasimha Reddy for their invaluable help in many walks of my life.

I take this opportunity to thank Smt. Yellapu Satyavathi, Dr. Chadaram Bala Krishna, Smt. C. Venkata Laxmi, Sri C. Naga Abhilash, Sri Yellapu Ramana, Y. Vimala, Dr. Y. Vikas, Sri Y. Abhishek, Sri Samineni Srinivasa Rao, Smt. Samineni Sandhya, Sri Buddha Srinivasa Rao, Smt. Buddha Vani Jahnavi, Dr. Buddha Veera Raghava Rao, Sri Samineni Papa Rao, Sri Hanumanthu Srinivasa Rao, Sri Buddha Prakash, Sri Dadi Appa Rao, Sri Saragadam Satyanarayana, Sri Vegi Surya Prakasa Rao, Dr Malla Appa Rao, Sri Polamarasetty Ramakrishna, Sri Yellapu Sivaji, Sri Yellapu Bujji, Sri Boddeti Tata Rao, Sri Kothari Ranga Rao, Sri Gurram Subba Rao, who were of immense help to me in many of my personal and social activities.

I thank Sri Jampana Prathap and Sri Pandu Yadav, leaders of our locality and Sri V. V. Ramana, Sri J. Chennakesavulu, Sri B. Malliah, Sri K. Chandra Sekhar

Reddy and other residents of our colony, who stood by me through thick and thin.

I commemorate with respect my father C. S. Naidu, mother C. Chinatalli, mother's elder sister C. Veeramma, Polamarasetty Appa Rao, Buddha Veeru Naidu, B. R. Satyanarayana, Karri Ramachandra Rao, Kothari Prakasa Rao, Kothari Kamalamma, Mudigonda Linga Murthy, D. Yashwanth Rao, V. Ramachandra Rao, Madeti Samba Murthy, Karra Venkata Subba Rao, Karri Satyanarayana Reddy and Tangi Sriramulu.

I thank readers, who provided valued feedback on books published by me earlier. I find no words to express how deeply I am impressed with dedicated support that I have received from staff of M/s Partridge Publishing.

I fail in my duty, if I don't express my heartfelt thanks to my wife Smt. C. L. Rajakumari, without the support of whom, I could not have remained in the field of writing.

PREFACE

This book is a sequel to my first book 'Telling Tales for Rising Stars' and the second in a series of books on telling tales. It is a collection of 125 micro tales, written keeping in view mainly young adults and those that take delight in reading thought stirring and enlightening literary works. Every tale in this book dwells on a crystal of thought and drives home a pointed message that makes readers think. The book as a whole is written for a purpose that is to give an idea on how we can live a life better than what we are living and how we can live holistically with enlarged horizon of thinking.

Before release of my first book into market, I had no idea as to how readers would receive my book. I was restless, until I received the first feedback from a reader. When some more readers read, reviewed and ratified quality of content in my book, I really got gratified and found myself standing on cloud nine. A word of appreciation from Principal of a high school that she read my book and recommended reading of the book to her students, filled me with euphoria. I have envisaged writing this book, after uplifting feedback from readers has given me confidence that I can continue in the field of writing.

I am a farmer by birth, an engineer by profession and a writer by instinct. I always toil and till my land of words to engineer crowning crops. If harvest from my first crop has found place in the form of telling tales in my first book, harvest from my second crop is finding place in the present book.

I have taken the route of expressing myself through writing extremely small short stories for three explicit reasons. The first reason is a modern reader, hard pressed for time, prefers reading short works to going through long works. The second reason is I have many ideas and concepts to share with my readers and I can do it only through writing small and short works, keeping brevity in mind. The third reason is a message from a writer reaches a reader more effectively through a story rather than through what is conveyed directly.

I have sincerely endeavoured to put together many of my thoughts in the form of tiny tales in the present book. I earnestly hope that the tales will provide good, light and healthy reading material for my readers. I also wish the book will delight the elite and erudite in the literary world and earn their admiration.

Author

FOREWORD

 From the beginning, man has lived with deep desire to have long, healthy and happy life. He has worked constantly towards realization of his cherished desire, hit upon many nuggets of knowledge and preserved them in the form of literature and science. If literature is contributing directly for enhancement of happiness through entertainment and enlightenment, science is doing it indirectly through taking care of health and creating many material comforts.

The author, an engineer with long drawn industrial experience, has combined science and literature to share his work and real life experiences through telling tales, with modern readers, hard pressed for time.

Most of the stories in this book reflect autographs of the author. They stand to highlight that work spot is a temple, founder of an organization is no way inferior to god, work is the only way to become great in life, time is to be utilized optimally, live and let live concept is to be respected, it is possible to address complex problems through out of the box thinking, every individual has self respect, responsible parenting is required to bring up children, taking care of society is a bounden duty of one and all, belief moves mountains, barbarous acts of bloodshed are bad, conscientious efforts are to be made to remove discords among family members and many more mind stirring thoughts. The stories, narrated in simple and lucid style, are sure to entertain readers with their crisp and clear messages.

The author has to his credit a few more good works. I am sure that the present compilation too will get good name and fame for him. I look forward for more publications from the author.

Dr. Bala Krishna Chadaram
Professor at Malla Reddy Medical College for
Women, Hyderabad,
Former Principal of RIMS, Kadapa

INTRODUCTION

Short stories in this book are small in size, but big in effect. They are carved out of crystals of thought. They are cast out of moulds to take shape into majestic pieces of art. They are tales of all times. They are impregnated with ideas. They are designed to deliver food for thought. They are handpicked both from real life incidents as well as realms of imagination.

They are crafted for a purpose. They make us realize what vast potential is there within us, how we can tap it and climb up to top notch positions in life. They drive away self defeating thoughts that swarm around us and dissuade us from undertaking anything worthwhile in life. They pull us out of self centred world and make us interface more harmoniously with outside society. They take out negativity from our minds and replace it with positivity. They make us see what shortcomings we have got in our personality and tell how we can do away with them. They lay emphasis on importance of work in life and highlight how work and success in life are interconnected. They tell us how good beliefs strengthen our spirits and wrong beliefs cut into our self confidence. They advocate how free and rational thinking helps and why we should have scientific bent of mind. They draw our attention to ever deteriorating human relations and make us feel the need to mend them. They tell in unequivocal terms that self is the supreme body in making success in life and all external help is only a supplement to it.

They teach us to learn good things, preach to us merits of morals and virtues in life and elucidate what happens, if we cross our limits, transgress into forbidden zones and commit wrongs that we are not supposed to attempt.

They are guides. They take us on a visit to various sightseeing spots in a conducted tour. They are magicians. They show in mirrors in their hands various glimpses of life. They are presenters. They introduce us to various characters and concepts picked out from various walks of life. They are pathfinders. They show us path to follow, before us. They are emitters of light. They conduct us from darkness into light. They are treasures of truth. They escalate us from what is unreal to real. They are springs of nectar. They take us from mortality to immortality. They are scintillating stars in a star studded sky. They send out golden sheens and make their presence felt. They are troves of wisdom. They elevate us from abysmal state of ignorance to higher level of learning. They are movers. They move us from inaction into action. They are chargers. They fill us with energy and enthusiasm.

There are some tales in this book that point out weaknesses in human nature. They are not written to find faults in others, but to spot the fault lines and find solutions for them.

There are many seasoned raconteurs in the tales. The raconteurs in the form of counsellors, gods, god men, kings, mentors, parents, peers, teachers, saints, seers and many other characters enter stage, one after another, narrate tales and exit in quick succession.

Tales in this book, an eclectic mix, arranged into a bouquet, are set to amuse, ameliorate, educate, enlighten, enthuse, enthral and inspire readers.

1. A GREAT VOCALIST

A young vocalist started her singing career with a good band of accompanists in her team. With devotion to music and dedication to profession, she won hearts of millions of music lovers. She continued her musical journey for a life time and established for herself great name and unparalleled fame. Throughout her journey, she never made any change in her ensemble. The accompanists that were in her team in beginning of her career, continued to be there in the team, all throughout. The musician took care of members of her team more than those of her own family. She was so noble that she gave away most of her earnings to her team mates and kept to herself very little.

Once, a media person wanted to write a report on musical odyssey of the accomplished musician. He met the musician, put a series of questions to her and said to her, at end of the interview:

"I understand that you take care of members of your team, a very great way."

"I do as much as I can do. They are my forte," said the musician.

"I understand that you distribute most of your earnings as hefty giveaways liberally to your associates," said the media person.

"I like to do so," said the musician.

"It is a great wonder to know that you have not kept anything for yourself and gave everything away to them," said the media person.

"Who can say that I have not kept anything for myself," said the musician.

"What did you keep for yourself?" said the media person.

"My team," said the musician.

2. ADVANCE BOOKING

A man admitted his aged father in an old age home. His father pleaded with his son not to do so. But the son did not heed. He left his father to himself and went away home. The father was desolate. But he was helpless. He learnt to live alone in the company of others in the home.

The home had a facility. It created employment to inmates of the house, in case the inmates desired to work. The father desired to work. The home created employment for him. The father worked, earned something out of his work and saved the earnings in a bank.

Many years passed. One fine morning, the son received news that his father was no more. He went to the home, collected body of his father, brought it home and finished the funeral rites. Next day, when he went to the home to collect left out belongings of his father from the home, manager of the home handed over a sealed cover to him and said:

"Please take this."

"What is it?" said the son.

"It contains advance booking papers," said the manager.

"I don't understand what it is," said the son.

"Your father, during his stay here, worked and earned. He spent his earnings to reserve a room in the old age home. The sealed cover contains receipt for payment made by your father and papers for advance booking of the room," said the manager.

"But why did my father book a room in the old age home?" said the son.

"For you," said the manager.

3. FORBIDDEN GORGE

A man had a brick kiln in a field close to a river. Every day, he went to the kiln to oversee brick making operations going on there. On one occasion, he was required to go to a distant place, for about a month, on some personal errand. He called his son and said:

"It will take about a month for me to return. During my absence, go regularly to the kiln and supervise operations there."

"I shall do it," said the son compliantly.

"I have to warn you about something," said the father.

"What is it?" said the son.

"There is a dangerous gorge behind our kiln, nearby the river. Never ever enter it. It is a forbidden place," said the father.

"What is dangerous about it?" queried the son.

"There are overhanging spirits in it. They could overpower intruders with their charms, take them over under their control, hold sway over them and literally transport them to hell," said the father.

The son agreed to comply with instructions of his father. The kiln owner went on his errand. The teenager son started going to the kiln. One day, the son went to the kiln, right in the morning, and put the workers in their places of work. Some workers dug soil and heaped it in a place. Some put water in the soil and made a wet mass out of it. Some put it in wooden moulds and cast raw bricks out of them. Some arrayed the bricks in rows and dried them under sun. Some arranged the dried bricks in pyramidal shapes, with provisions for series of kilns underneath for fire. Some cut logs, put them in the kilns and set them on fire. The son oversaw the operations, going on at the site until noon, and went to backside of the kiln to go to the riverside.

He went to the riverside, spent some time there, in cool running water of the river, and suddenly called back to memory what his father said about the gorge nearby. He shuddered with fear to think of the spirits said to be hanging around in the gorge. But he could not suppress curiosity to see what was there in the gorge. Slowly and cautiously, he walked towards the gorge that sprawled close by, off the riverside and dared enter it. He was on a lookout for the dreaded spirits that could be hiding in the surroundings. But he saw nothing. He moved forward. When he passed along through the wide, wooded and winding gorge, he suddenly noticed some scenes of obscenity in dusky and secluded spots in surroundings of the gorge. A catchy scene attracted attention of the teenager and he stood still, without stirring and looking hooked to the scene. The boy was charmed. He could not turn his eyes off the scene. He stood at the place until the scene melted out of his sight and he dragged his feet back to his place of work.

The boy, drawn magnetically by the sight that came into his view the day before, went into the grove, the next day too, looking out for scenes similar to what he saw the day before. And he continued to do so, until his father returned after one month.

The kiln owner came to know from his workers that his son frequented the grove every day and it cost a huge effort for him to stop his son from going into the seductive gorge, inhabited by charmers.

4. SELECTION

A king conducted a test for selection of new recruits for his army. He designated a renowned warrior for selection of the recruits. Many candidates from far and near of the kingdom flocked to the centre of selection.

The selector was very strict in his selection. He fixed criteria for selection and tried to select aspirants as per the criteria. The selection process continued for many days. After end of the test process, the selector declared that no one was selected for the army. The king was surprised. He said nothing to the selector. But he called his chief minister and said to him:

"I am astonished to hear that no candidate is found suitable for selection into army. Are our job aspirants so bad? What shall we do?"

"Be pleased to permit me to handle the issue," said the chief minister.

The king permitted the chief minister. The chief minister changed selector and re-conducted the test for selection. The second selector conducted the test and selected as many candidates as were required for the army. When the chief minister took the selection list to the king, the king exclaimed:

"Please explain how the first selector failed to select candidates and the second one succeeded?"

"The first selector is a warrior of high excellence. He looked out for warrior qualities of high standard, which were great in his looks, in the aspirants, and found none fit for selection. The second selector looked out for warrior qualities that the amateur young aspirants could showcase and found many fit for the selection," said the chief minister.

The king appreciated wisdom of his chief minister and approved of the selection list.

5. POLLUTION

A learned man, who settled in a foreign land, heard a lot about a river that was in his homeland. He heard that the river was very holy and taking a dip in it was highly auspicious. He developed a strong desire to take a dip in the river. But, because of his preoccupations and by being away from his homeland by a long distance, he could not make it happen. The desire in him remained as a desire and it never materialized.

Mother of the man passed away. Before her death, she asked her son to take her ashes back to his homeland and put them into the river that he dreamt of taking a dip in. The man knew that it was a difficult task. But he decided to honour last words of his mother. He collected ashes from mortal remains of his mother, flew to his homeland, travelled to the place where the river flowed, went to the riverside, walked knee deep into the river water, offered salutations in reverence to the river that occupied space in his mind for decades and mixed ashes of his mother into the river. He turned back. He did not take a dip in the holy river. The river was highly polluted.

6. MISER

Every day evening, when a commuter got down from his bus at a market place and walked briskly towards his home, he saw a beggar craving for alms by roadside.

Whenever he saw the beggar, he felt like giving him small change, put his hand into his trouser pocket to take it out, and, invariably, he passed by the beggar, without taking out anything and parting with it to the beggar. He felt bad for his action. But he consoled himself by thinking that he could do it, the next day. Days, weeks and months passed. But the next day did never come. The man never gave alms to the beggar.

One day, when the man alighted from his bus and went towards his home, passing by the beggar, the beggar asked for alms. The man, habitually and invariably, put his hand into his pocket and found to his dismay that there was no change in the pocket. He felt very happy. He told himself that he really wanted to give some change to the beggar and unfortunately there was no change in his pocket. He thought how good it could be if there was no money in his pocket, whenever he put his hand into his pocket to take it out.

7. THE VEGETABLE VENDOR

Every day, a vegetable vendor, a middle aged woman, with a basket of vegetables on her head, went to a newly developed residential colony, moved from house to house in the colony, announced her arrival by shouting what vegetables she had, and sold her vegetables. The homemakers in the colony eagerly waited for her coming, stopped her in front of their houses and bought vegetables from her. By midday, the vendor sold off her vegetables, went to a district bus stand nearby and went back to her village, a few miles away. She lived happily on what she earned out her small scale sales.

Over the years, the colony expanded. Population of residents increased. A series of shops selling grocery, vegetables and other commodities needed by the local residents came up in the colony. People, who patronized the vegetable vendor for over two decades, stopped buying from her and turned to buying from the vegetable shop. The vendor lost her livelihood. Often, she went back home with vegetables in her basket unsold. But still, she did not stop visiting the colony to sell her vegetables.

One noon, when it was very hot outside, the vendor lowered her basket in front of a house and said to the householder lady that stood in veranda of the house:

"Mother, I am feeling very thirsty. Will you please give me some water to drink?"

The householder gave the vendor water. The vendor drank the water and thanked lady of the house. The householder looked at the basket, full of vegetables, and said to the vendor:

"Did you not sell your vegetables today? The basket is still full."

"Nobody has bought vegetables from me. Probably, I shall have to take them back," said the vendor.

"You are looking very tired. Come inside and rest for a while," said the householder.

"I cannot do it. I have to move to other areas to sell my vegetables," said the vendor.

"Did you have something to eat?" said the householder.

"I have not brought food. I shall go back and have it at home," said the vendor.

"It will be nightfall by the time you go back home for lunch. Come inside. I shall serve you some food," said the householder.

The vendor was hungry. She did not object to the householder. The householder took the vendor inside compound of her house, made her sit, spread a leaf before her and served food. The vendor took the food gratefully. After a while, the vendor took a handful of vegetables from her basket, gave lady of the house and said:

"I shall be very happy, if you take these vegetables," said the vendor.

"How much shall I pay for them?" said the householder.

"Don't pay me anything," said the vendor.

"Are you paying me back for my food?" said the householder.

"That, I can never do. Although you are very young, you served me food and treated me like a mother. As a token of gratitude, I am offering these vegetables to you. I shall be very happy, if you take them," said the vendor.

The householder was touched. She understood feelings of the vendor and took the vegetables. She did not pay for the vegetables. But she said to the vendor:

"From tomorrow onwards, come to me daily. I shall buy vegetables from you."

8. NEIGHBOURS

Two friends, a trader and a farmer, built their houses, side by side, in a residential colony. They remained like friends only for some time. After that, for some petty reason, differences cropped up between them. They grew day by day and led to frequent fights. For every silly reason, the trader picked up argument with the farmer and called him names. Initially, the farmer did not tolerate indecent behaviour of the trader. He got angry and reacted sharply. But when the arguments and consequential worded fights became order of the day, the farmer understood that he could not continue to live the way he lived, with no peace of mind. He worked out a solution to avoid argument with his peevish neighbour. Every day, right in the morning, the farmer along with his wife left home, went to his fields, spent his time there until the day was over and returned home only after nightfall. When this continued for a long time, the trader did not get opportunity to meet his farmer neighbour and pick up an argument with him. He boiled with rage, but could do nothing.

The farmer and his wife virtually converted their house into a rest house for the night. They spent most of their time only in their fields and grew crops of various varieties. With their devoted work, they took out maximum yield from their fields and drew attention of a local landlord. The landlord, in appreciation of the great yield that the farmer took from his field, arranged a felicitation ceremony, attended by many farmers from the surrounding villages, and said to the farmer:

"You have taken yield from your field more than anyone in our entire neighbourhood. Please tell what the secret of your high yield is."

"My good trader neighbour," said the farmer.

9. TWENTY FOUR HOURS

A landlord in a village was merciless. He exploited labourers badly. He took labourers on contract, employed them in his fields and made them work continuously throughout the day, with no rest in between. If any labourer refused to honour his command, he mercilessly imposed cuts in wages to be paid to him. For fear of loss of wages, no labourer dared talk against the landlord. Local labourers, who knew nature of the landlord, did not show interest to work with the landlord. The land lord mostly took on contract non-local labourers that knew nothing about his exploitive nature.

Headman of the village received many complaints against the landlord. But he did not get a chance to fix the landlord. The landlord was very careful in framing of rules of his contract. The headman waited for a chance to teach a lesson to the landlord. One day, he got a chance. The landlord unwittingly walked into a big trap. He met the headman and said:

"I want your help."

"Tell me what way I can help you?" said the headman.

"I want to take a labourer on contract for one year. I wish to finalise the deal in your presence," said the landlord.

"What is special about the deal?" said the headman.

"I have a labourer who wants to work all the twenty four hours. I want to take him into service," said the landlord.

"Is the labourer prepared to work all the twenty four hours?" said the headman.

"Yes. He is prepared," said the landlord.

The headman called the labourer standing at a distance and asked him if he was prepared to work for all the twenty four hours. The labourer confirmed. The headman gave a green signal for the deal. The deal was struck instantaneously. The land lord, very happy after the deal, went away with the labourer following him.

Within a week, the trouble started. There started disagreement between the landlord and his new recruit. The landlord went back to the headman with his new recruit standing behind him and lodged a complaint against the labourer. He said:

"I want to cut wages of this labourer for his breach of contract."

"What way did he breach the contract?" said the headman.

"This man, in your presence earlier, has committed to work for all the twenty four hours. But he is not respecting his commitment," said the landlord.

"What do you say for it?" said the headman, looking at the labourer.

"I am working for all the twenty four hours as committed by me," said the labourer.

"This man is working for twenty four hours a week, not a day," said the landlord.

"I never said that I would work twenty four hours a day," said the labourer.

"I am sorry. I can do nothing to help you in this case. There is nothing for me to find fault with the labourer. Before entering into agreement with him, you should have verified whether the twenty four hours were per day or week," said the headman.

"What shall I do now?" said the landlord.

"Come to terms with the labourer and wriggle out of the situation gracefully," said the headman.

The landlord cursed himself for his foolhardiness. He followed advice of the headman and settled dispute with the labourer amicably. He lost a lot in the deal. He learnt a lesson, a hard way. He stopped exploiting his employees. The headman never revealed that he engineered the deal to teach the landlord a lesson.

10. THE HERO OF A MAN

A courtesan found a little boy of one year sitting on footsteps of her house and crying. She took pity on the boy, lifted him into her hands and took him inside her house. She made enquiries about the boy. But she got no clue about who left the boy on doorsteps of her house. She decided to raise the boy under her care and kept the boy in her house. She liked the boy. She showered her love on the little toddler. An old maid in service of the courtesan observed her mistress for a few days and said to her:

"You are dotting on the boy very much."

"I love to do it," said the courtesan.

"What do you want to do with the boy?" said the maid.

"I want to raise him as my son," said the courtesan.

"And you want him to be looked down upon by society as son of a courtesan," said the maid.

"I don't want that to happen," said the courtesan.

"If it is so, leave the boy in a place where he can grow honourably," said the maid.

The courtesan took clue from the old maid. She felt very sad to leave the boy. But she found logic in what her maid said. She thought and thought and took a hard decision. She took the boy to a priest in a local temple and said to him:

"Sir, I came to request you for a favour."

"What do you want?" said the priest.

"I found this boy on door steps of my house. I wanted to raise him as my son. But I do not want to do it. I shall be grateful, if you will raise the boy on my behalf. I shall give you as much money as you want," said the courtesan.

"But, why don't you raise the boy yourself?" said the priest.

"I do not want to do it," said the courtesan.

"Why?" said the priest.

"I am a courtesan. I do not want the boy to become son of a courtesan," said the courtesan.

The priest was touched. He acceded to request of the courtesan. He refused money offered by the courtesan and said:

"Leave the boy with me."

The courtesan left the boy with the priest. The priest did not keep the boy with him. He took the boy to a school in a far away forest and admitted him in the school, as his own son. He visited the school now and again and enquired about how the boy fared in the forest school. He sent periodically messages to the courtesan on how her son fared in the school.

Many years passed. King of the land died in a battle. A new king occupied the throne. The new ruler brought many changes in political system for welfare of his subjects.

One day, the priest met the courtesan in her house and asked her to accompany with him, on a pilgrimage trip. The courtesan was taken aback for such a request from the priest. She obliged the request instantly. The priest took the courtesan to a place, where a horse drawn carriage awaited. Both got into the carriage and the carriage set off. The carriage went to the fort, from which the new king ruled. Guards at gateway of the fort received the guests with utmost respect and conducted them into presence of the king in his private chamber of the palace. The king saw the priest, got up and offered his salutations to the priest. The priest blessed the king, showed him the courtesan beside him and said:

"Meet your mother."

The king fell prostrate at feet of his mother and fell into her embrace. Next day, in court hall, in presence of all courtiers, elite and erudite, the king announced proudly that he got his mother after many years of separation and he showed his mother to people in the hall.

11. SKIING

A man watched his teenage sons, skiing on a snow covered mountainside. He liked the way his sons negotiated curves around obstacles on way and manoeuvred down the hill. He got enthused to ski. But he could not risk the sport, since he was not trained in it. He expressed to his sons that he too wanted to ski and enjoy the sport. His sons took him to a coach and asked him to learn the art, under able guidance of the coach. The father was thrilled. He started learning the sport under personal supervision of the coach.

The man took quite some time to learn skiing, due to his age. But, by and by, he picked it up. However, he skied, only when the coach was closely around. For fear of a fatal fall, he never skied, in the absence of the coach.

One day, the coach asked the man to ski. He told his ward to try it independently. When the man hesitated, he said to the man:

"Have no fear. I am here to take care of you. Ski and show me how perfect you have become."

"If you are close by around, I can try it," said the man.

"I shall not stir from where I am now," said the coach.

The man, with the confidence that his coach was close by, attempted his feat downhill, along a safe path, and reached end of the path successfully. He was thrilled at success of his first independent attempt and looked up at the coach watching from top of the hill. He got panicky. He noticed that the coach was not there in his place. He got angry with the coach. But, very soon, he turned jubilant. The very thought that he could ski independently made him euphoric and saw him floating on air.

12. SHRINE

Every day, the son of a sand supplier went along with his father to a rivulet, inside a forest, to dig sand from the riverbed and load in a bullock cart. One day, he found cute rock idol of a deity buried underneath the sand. He took out the idol with ecstasy and showed to his father. On the advice of his father, he took the idol into a pool of water in the rivulet, washed it in the water, took it away to a huge tree on banks of the rivulet and installed the idol on an elevated pedestal underneath the tree. Next day, he brought from home turmeric powder and vermilion and anointed the idol with them. He worshipped the goddess reverentially, regularly and ritualistically, whenever he went to the riverside for transportation of sand.

Many years passed. During the period, the sand supplier changed his profession, left the village, where he stayed for long years, went away to a far off town and started a new business. Son of the sand supplier went to school in the town, studied well, secured a job in service of king of the land and became a big officer.

One day, the officer happened to go on official visit to a far off land. On the way, villagers from a village met the officer and invited him to visit their village. The officer obliged request of the villagers and went inside their village. Headman of the village received the officer with utmost courtesy, treated him well with warm hospitality and requested him to visit a famous shrine in suburbs of the village. The officer agreed. The headman conducted the officer and his subordinate staff to the shrine. The officer went inside the shrine, offered his prayers to the presiding deity and relaxed for a while, in open yard before the shrine. The headman said to the officer:

"I want to tell you something special about this shrine."

"What is it?" said the officer.

"The deity here appeared all of a sudden from nowhere to bless our land. Once in every one year, we hold a great fair in name of the goddess. People from far and near throng to see the goddess during the festival time," said the headman.

"That is great," said the officer.

After visit to the temple, the officer along with his staff proceeded away, on his way. He chose not to reveal that idol in the shrine was installed by him.

13. PARTIALITY

An officer in a factory was highly work minded. He worked hard and expected his staff to equally work hard. He did not hesitate to take action against anyone, who showed signs of indiscipline in work area. He was conspicuous in one area. He never took action against his personal assistant, who was good at work, but undisciplined, at times.

Some people in the department, who were against authoritative nature of the officer, turned against him and attributed to him motive of partiality. They complained to a senior officer, under whom the officer worked, that the officer did not treat all alike and he was particularly partial to his personal assistant. The senior officer called the officer to his cabin and asked for explanation for his soft corner towards his personal assistant. He said:

"I am told that you are highly partial towards your personal assistant."

"That I am, sir," said the officer.

"Partiality is not good. Avoid it," said the senior officer.

"I cannot avoid it," said the officer.

"Why?" said the senior officer, turning serious.

"Because my personal assistant works," said the officer.

The senior officer said no more. He melted down from seriousness into broad smile. The officer left the cabin and went away to do his job.

14. HOUSE PLAN

A householder constructed a new house and performed house warming ceremony in it. After occupying the house, wife of the householder observed that some incidents, supposed to be due to ill luck, occurred in her family circle and she attributed them to unlucky aspect of the house. She asked her husband to bring a consultant, who knew how to remove ill luck associated with the house. The householder did not do what his wife asked him to do for a long time. But, pestered once and again by his wife and finding no escape, he went finally to a popular consultant, who advertised for himself that he knew the art of driving away ill luck associated with houses. He brought the consultant to his house and showed him layout of the house.

The consultant studied how various rooms in the house plan were configured, which direction main entrance of the house faced and relevant aspects required for the study and gave his expert opinion on the house. He concluded that the house plan had many fault lines that brought ill luck to occupants of the house and suggested for extensive modifications to be carried out to correct the fault lines. He took his hefty consultation fee and went away.

The house owner was worried. He studied recommendations of the consultant and observed that in case he went for implementation of recommendations of the consultant, he would have to bring down the structure in its present configuration and raise a new structure in place of it. He shuddered at the very thought of going for the alterations that would cost a fortune. He put aside the recommendations and did nothing to make any change in the house. Lady of the house did not take action of her husband lightly. She said to her husband:

"I am amazed at your callousness. You are not taking any action on recommendations of the consultant. Tell plainly what is there in your mind."

"I do not want to act on the recommendations," said the house owner coldly.

"Why?" said lady of the house.

"Cost of alterations is as high as building a new house," said the house owner.

"It is just nothing, considering loss due to calamities that we have suffered so far and we are likely to suffer in future, in consequence of unlucky aspect of the house," said lady of the house.

"I don't believe that there is any correlation between the house and the calamities," said the house owner.

"I believe," said lady of the house.

"What shall I do, then?" said the house owner.

"Go for the alterations," said lady of the house.

"Look. I am not going to do it. I am not so rich that I can afford to go for the changes suggested by the consultant. I wish to draw your attention to the fact that before construction of this house, we have consulted a consultant and we built the house as per his recommendations, supposed to usher in good luck to us. When recommendations of the first consultant failed to yield good luck to us, how should I take it for granted that recommendations of the second consultant will bring good luck to us?" said the house owner.

"I agree with what you say. But we can find a via media solution for this," said lady of the house.

"What is it?" said the house owner.

"Let us bring a third consultant and take his opinion," said lady of the house.

"I can do it on one condition," said the house owner.

"What is it?" said lady of the house.

"If recommendations of the third consultant are in matching with those of the second consultant, I shall undertake the alterations immediately. Otherwise you must drop the idea of making changes in the house," said the house owner.

"Agreed," said lady of the house.

"Suggest whom shall we bring as a third consultant," said the house owner.

Lady of the house suggested name of a consultant, about whom she heard a lot from her neighbours. The house owner went straight to the third consultant, brought him home, showed him the house, took his opinion on alterations to be effected in presence of his wife, paid fee and saw the consultant off.

After the third consultant left, the house owner and his wife went through his recommendations, compared them with recommendations of the second consultant and noticed that there was no match between one lot and the other. Lady of the house realized, though lately, that she unnecessarily made her husband run after consultants, who gave incongruous reports that conflicted with each other. He bothered her husband no more for alterations in the house.

15. MARRIAGE ALLIANCE

A downtrodden section of society suffered heavily under oppressive regime of a king. A young leader from the section championed the cause of his community and fought against oppressive regime of king of the land. He, with support of many other people that were poised against the king, threw the king out of power, and became king of the land.

Years passed. Daughter of the new king attained marriageable age. The new king wanted to search for a suitable match for his daughter. He called his chief minister and said to him:

"Please search out for a good match for the princess."

"I shall do it," said the chief minister.

"Look out for a good match from within my community," said the king.

"This instant, I shall detail alliance makers to go to your native place and search out for a good match for the princess," said the chief minister.

"Why do you want to send the alliance makers to my native place?" said the king.

"That is where your community is there," said the chief minister.

"I don't belong to the community that you are referring to," said the king.

"What community do you belong to?" said the chief minister.

"The community of kings," said the king.

16. NO WAR TREATY

A king fought many wars, conquered all kingdoms in the world and brought them under his sovereign rule. He ruled the world, all throughout his life. At end of his life, he left the world and went to upper worlds. Many generations passed. The king developed a strong desire to see the world that he ruled, at one point of time in the past. He heard that a descendant from his family ruled the empire, left behind by him. He left his place in the upper world, where he lived, and descended to earth. He toured entire earth, went from kingdom to kingdom and felt jubilant to note that perfect peace prevailed in every part of earth. He was very happy to observe that the peace that he established after a series of wars still continued and perfect amity made place among kingdoms that constituted his erstwhile empire. He went to the capital, from where he ruled in the past and his descendant ruled in the present, met the descendant in his palace, introduced himself and said:

"I came here to congratulate you."

"What for do you want to congratulate me?" said the descendant king.

"I want to congratulate you, because you are successfully continuing the rich legacy that I have left behind," said the departed king.

"What is the rich legacy that you have left behind?" said the descendant king.

"I fought many wars, brought all kingdoms in the world under my control and established peace in the world. I am delighted to notice that the peace which I left behind is still prevailing in the world," said the departed king.

"There is peace in the world. But it is not the peace that you left behind. It is peace of different nature," said the descendant king.

"What is it?" said the departed king.

"The peace, not following wars but resulting out of no war treaties with neighbouring kingdoms," said the descendant king.

The king looked at his descendant in dismay and lifted himself back to the place that he descended from.

17. REPORTER'S REPORT

Violent communal riots took place in sensitive part of a city. Two communities that lived together in the area with amity for centuries suddenly turned against each other, over a petty issue and fought pitched battles. They charged at each other with lethal weapons and caused extensive damage to human life and material properties. The violence cost many human lives and the death toll rose steadily.

A junior reporter, working for a news paper, went to the area of violence, to take stock of the situation prevailing there and report precisely how many people lost their lives in the mindless violence. He was shocked. He came to know that magnitude of the violence was much more than what was reported earlier. First hand reports from people, who witnessed the violence, confirmed that dozens of people lost their lives in the riots and there were many casualties from both the warring sides.

He went back to his desk, prepared a comprehensive report on the violence and submitted it to his boss, with all supporting documents. The boss, a seasoned reporter, sifted through the detailed report, edited it and released it to the press. When the report appeared in newspaper, the next day, the junior reporter went hurriedly through it, went to his boss and said:

"I am surprised."

"What happened?" said the senior reporter.

"There is no comparison between what I reported yesterday and what has come out in paper today," said the junior reporter.

"You are right," said the senior reporter.

"But why my report is not published as it is? I have taken lot of pains to collect information about how many people died from each community, how the trouble started and who are black sheep that have triggered the riots. What is reported in paper today hardly reflects what I have reported. On the other hand, news in the paper says that peace is fast returning to the strife torn area. I would like to know who has changed my report," said the junior reporter, pain struck.

"I have done it," said the senior reporter, coolly

"Why did you do it?" said the junior reporter, sounding impatient.

"Not reporting facts is better than reporting facts in certain cases. Had the report, prepared by you, appeared in newspaper today, it would have led to further escalation of tensions between the warring communities. Hiding truth is good for society in some situations. That is why, I hid the truth from common public surcharged with emotions," said the senior reporter.

The junior reporter appreciated viewpoint of his boss. He learnt how to report under guidance of his expert boss and rose to become a great reporter in course of time.

18. KING'S DILEMMA

Intelligence reports reached a king that some rebels worked actively to cause wide spread disturbances in his state. They also brought in tidings that some foreign elements teamed up with internal rebels to destabilise his rule. The king got alert. He took action to crack down upon trouble makers in his state and put a check on their mutinous activities.

When things started improving, suddenly there was an attempt on his life. The king received it as a big jolt. Investigation into the incident revealed that some inmates of the palace were behind the incident and they worked at the behest of some opponents that connived to eliminate the king. The king could not digest the incident. He was never unjust in his rule. He was fair to everyone. He could not understand how his own staff in palace colluded with conspirators outside. He was deeply hurt. He called his chief minister and said:

"I have not harmed anybody. Still some people are after my life. What has happened once may repeat again. I do not want this to happen. I want to leave the throne."

The chief minister was a seasoned administrator. He thought for a while and said to the king:

"Sir, you are disturbed after the incident. I can imagine what is passing in your mind. I too feel that you should not remain in the palace for some time. Go on a tour to some unknown places for some time and come back. If you will still hold the view that you cannot sit on the throne, then we shall decide upon what to do. Go in the guise of a common traveller, through one of the underground passages leading out of the palace."

The king had high respect for his chief minister. He acted on his advice and left the palace, all at once, through a secret passage. He proceeded on a long journey, moving from place to place. A few months passed.

One day, when the king was on his way, under scorching sun, he felt very thirsty. He looked out for a possible source of water. He spotted a well in a way side field at a distance. A man drew water through a perforated bucket that worked on a pulley system. A bullock, moving to front and back, operated the rope tied to the bucket. The king was thrilled. He dismounted his horse and walked to the well, along with his horse. The bucket, which brought out water from the well, emptied it out into an open duct, carved out of a palm log, and the water flowed into a nearby field. A farmer along with his wife worked in the field. The king quenched his thirst, left the horse there to drink water and went inside field to greet the farmer. The king said to the farmer:

"What are you doing?"

"I am taking out weeds from the field," said the farmer.

"Even if you take them out, they will grow again," said the king.

"I have to weed them out, whenever they will grow. Otherwise, they will not allow my crop to grow," said the farmer.

"How many times do you do so?" said the king.

"I don't mind doing it any number of times. Protecting my crop is my prime responsibility. If I don't take out weeds, every now and then, and ensure that my crop grows well, I am not fit to be a farmer," said the farmer.

The king felt as if the farmer indirectly hinted at him. He got into thinking. He found instant answer for the predicament that he passed through. He thanked the farmer, put a stop to his aimless travel, returned to palace and took reins of rule back into his hands. He went in a big way to identify trouble creators that created spokes in his rule, got them rounded up, brought them to book and paved way for return of peace in his kingdom. He remembered forever what the farmer said. He looked out constantly for bad elements in his kingdom and weeded them out, whenever they raised their ugly heads and posed threat to his rule.

19. CAMARADERIE

Two lady workers worked for daily wages, with a building contractor. They reported for work right in the morning, worked until evening and returned home by nightfall. They were good friends. They lived side by side in a slum area. They moved together, wherever they went. They worked with the contractor for many years. They never absented from work and the contractor never disengaged them from service.

One day, when the lady workers worked at a construction site, one lady cracked a joke and the second lady started giggling. The contractor, who stood nearby, felt that the second lady laughed at him. He was offended. He was highly displeased. He dismissed the second lady from service, right away. The poor lady was taken aback. She broke into tears. The first lady intervened and requested the contractor not to be very harsh with the second lady. But the contractor stuck to his stand. He refused to reconsider his decision and asked the second lady to leave the site, at once. The second lady, half dead with shame and half dead with insult, left the site with tears rushing out of her eyes. The first lady did not take the act kindly. She continued her work until evening and went back home.

Next day, the first lady did not turn up for work. The contractor sent for her. The lady refused to report for work. The contractor did not like to lose a good worker. He went in person to house of the first lady. The first lady told him very politely that he dismissed the second lady from service, for no fault of her, and she would not agree to work with him, until he agreed to take the second lady into service. The contractor softened his stand. He called the second lady, apologised for his rudeness and took her back into service. Both the ladies thanked the contractor and went jubilantly with him to their place of work.

20. SELF ESTEEM

Two police officers went on duty to a tribal hamlet in a forest. They finished their job there and started back to head quarters by a police jeep. They travelled throughout the night and, by morning, stopped by a wayside restaurant for refreshments. They went inside the restaurant, a thatched hut, occupied a wooden bench by a side and ordered for what they wanted. A man took the order and supplied with what the officers ordered.

When the officers took the dishes served before them, a middle aged woman with her five year old son entered the hut and sat on a bench opposite to them. The woman ordered for a glass of tea and an empty glass. The server served the same. The woman poured out some tea in the empty glass and gave his son. But the son refused to take it. The woman cajoled. But the boy did not heed. The woman said in a low tone:

"Don't make a scene here. All are watching. Take tea. We have to rush out. I am to go a long way to my work place."

"I don't want tea. I am feeling hungry. I want to eat something," said the boy.

"I don't have money. I can't help you with eatables," said the woman.

"I am feeling hungry. I want to eat something," said the boy in tears.

"Take tea. I can't give you anything more," said the woman in hushed tone, trying not being heard by others.

The police officers, who watched the scene before them, were touched. One of them called the boy to his side and said:

"Ask for whatever you like to eat. I shall pay for it."

The boy looked up into face of the police officer and said:

"I do not want anything to eat."

"Are you not feeling hungry?" said the police officer.

"No," said the boy.

The boy went back to his mother, drank the tea shared by her, held her hand and walked with dignity out of the hut. Before leaving the hut, the boy looked again into the face of the police officer. The police officer saw a sparkle of self esteem in eyes of the little boy.

21. HEROES

A boy read many story books written by an author. He noticed that storylines in every book of the author were around heroes that performed heroic deeds. He wondered why storylines were built around only heroes and not other characters in society. He went to the author, who wrote the story books, and asked him:

"Sir, I have a doubt."

"Please ask," said the author.

"Storylines in all your story books revolve around only heroes in society. Why don't you choose commoners in society to build your storylines around?" said the boy.

"I have very little time," said the author.

"What do you mean? I am not getting you," said the boy.

"I hardly find time to write stories about heroes, who have a lot to say through their lives. Wherefrom should I get time to write stories about commoners, who have nothing to convey through their lives," said the author.

22. RESPONSIBLE PARENT

A young lady was very brilliant in her studies. She graduated from a college and tried hard to get selected for IAS, a coveted central service in a nation. She fell through her efforts. She settled down in a state government service that was less in status than what she tried for and started her working career. She worked hard and rose very fast in her career.

She was married. She had a son. She took all possible care to see that her son studied well. But she found that he required more personal care, which she could not afford, because of her busy service life. She thought of how best she could pay more personal attention on his son. But she got no way out. One fine morning, all of a sudden, she took decision to resign from her job and submitted resignation in her office. Her colleagues and superiors were stunned at her decision. Her associates admonished her for her hasty decision. Her boss called and counselled her:

"You took a wrong decision."

"I took a right decision, sir," said the lady.

"Do you know that you have bright future ahead of you?" said the boss.

"I know," said the lady.

"Know that you are going to become conferred IAS, a rare honour in state government service," said the boss.

"I know, sir," said the lady.

"Take my advice and take back your resignation," said the boss.

"Please excuse me, sir. I took a decision to quit the service and I do not like to reconsider that," said the lady.

The lady stuck to her decision and left a highly promising career. Everyone including her husband faulted her for the decision that she took. The lady did not repent. She dedicated her out of service time to her only son.

Her son under personal care of his mother did extremely well in studies. He tried for the same position what his mother tried for and failed, once upon a time. He succeeded in his very first attempt, with flying colours. When he broke the news to his mother, his mother jumped in joy. She was on cloud nine. She shed tears of happiness. She, overwhelmed with surge of joy, could hardly control herself. She shook hands with her son and said:

"I am happy. You have done it."

"It is all because of your sacrifice," said the moved son, inundated with gratefulness.

"I did not make any sacrifice," said the mother.

"Had you not resigned for me, you could have become a conferred IAS by now," said the son, looking into eyes of his mother.

"Had I not resigned, I could have become a conferred IAS at fag end of my service. Because I resigned, I am able to see my son as a coveted IAS, at very starting of his career,"

The son held head of his mother in his hands and imprinted a kiss on her forehead. Warm tears of joy streamed down cheeks of the ecstatic mother.

23. TWO STAGE WRITING

There lived a famous writer in a city. He followed a typical writing style. He never attempted to write anything, straightaway. Firstly, he collected thoughts on what he wanted to write, scribbled them on whatever loose papers that came within his reach and put them on his writing table. He did it until he assured for himself that he collected all thoughts for what he wanted to write. Lastly, after the collection was over, he put the papers before him, went through them from beginning to end and started writing what he wanted to write, by entering into a computer.

Papers, scribbled by the writer, every now and then, lay loosely on his table and presented an untidy look. One day, son of the writer commented:

"Don't you think that you are doing your writing two times and wasting your time? Instead, you can enter what you want to write straightaway into a computer and do away with writing on loose papers."

"I cannot do it," said the father.

"Why do you say so?" said the son.

"I cannot think and do, both activities at the same time," said the father.

"What do you mean?" said the son.

"When I am in thinking mode, I scribble on papers. When I am in working mode, I enter data into computer," said the father.

"I think you can download thoughts straight from your mind into computer, in a single go," said the son.

"I am not able to do it. You try it and tell me if you can do it," said the father.

The son tried a piece of writing. He thought of what to write, sat before a computer, entered what he wanted to write in the computer, took a printout of the writing and went through it. He was stunned. He noticed that what he wrote came out to be something wholly different from what he wanted to write. He shared his experience with his father and wondered how it happened. The writer said:

"When you think and write on a computer simultaneously, it is quite probable that what you write deviates from what you want to write. Scribbled notes before you obviate your writing from suffering the deviation."

Son of the writer understood why his father followed two stage writing and toed the same line to write. Eventually, he became as good a writer as his father.

24. TAKING ACTION

A young officer took charge of engineering department in a factory. The department discharged many functions. It coordinated with design engineers, prepared design drawings for products under design, built prototype units of the product, tried and tested them out, incorporated improvements in them, generated engineering drawings fit for regular production and liaised with manufacturing departments to resolve production related problems. The officer managed staff working in the department, who, by virtue of their disciplines, performed various kinds of jobs connected to the department.

The officer was extremely unhappy with one employee, who failed to do jobs assigned to him, effectively. He was cut up with the employee. He admonished the employee many times and advised him to improve his working. But the employee did not change for better.

One day, the officer entrusted a very important job to the employee and asked him to complete it urgently. The employee took up the job and made a mess of it. For fault of the employee, the officer faced ire from his higher up. He lost his patience. He went to his superior officer and complained to him against the employee. The superior said:

"What is the problem you are facing with your subordinate?"

"He is not doing work to my satisfaction," said the young officer.

"What do you propose to do with him?" said the superior.

"I want to take action against him," said the young officer.

"You may do so. But before that, do one thing," said the superior.

"What is it?" said the young officer.

"Move the employee from what he is doing to what he can do well," said the superior.

"How do I know what job he can do well?" said the young officer.

"Talk to him and know from him," said the superior.

The young officer was not happy with decision given by his boss. But he decided to go by his decision. He called the employee, with whom he had problem, to his cabin, talked to him, knew from him which area of the department he could work in more effectively and shifted him from the area where he was working to the area where he said he could work better.

The employee, who failed in his earlier work area, performed very well in his new work area and worked to satisfaction of his boss. He did not give chance to his boss to complain against him anymore.

25. SON

A middle aged farmer and his wife worked in their field. They drew out water from a water canal beside their field and watered crop in the field. They worked hard under hot sun and perspired profusely. A boy in his young teens saw the hard working couple from a distance, approached the couple hesitantly and said to the farmer:

"May I help you!"

"Who are you?" questioned the farmer.

"I am an orphan," said the boy.

"Don't you have anyone of your own?" said the farmer.

"No," said the boy.

"Which place do you hail from?" said the farmer.

"I don't know," said the boy.

"What do you want for your service?" said the farmer.

"Give me food to eat," said the boy.

"Did you take food today?" said the farmer.

"No," said the boy.

The farmer stopped work and asked his wife to serve food for the boy. The lady served food. The boy ate food and took place of the lady to draw water along with the farmer.

At end of the day, the farmer asked the boy if he wished to go with him to stay in his house. The boy agreed readily. He became a member of the farmer's family.

The farmer and his wife became old. They stopped going to field. The boy who turned into a young man took care of the farm. He never asked the farmer remuneration for his service and the farmer never offered the same for services of the young man.

The farmer became sick. He was on his death bed. He called the young man and said:

"I am going. Take care of my wife."

"That I shall do," said the young man.

Next day, the farmer passed away. Elders in the neighbourhood asked the lady:

"Who will light pyre of your husband."

"My son will do it," said the lady.

The elders were perplexed. They knew that the farmer couple had no issues. The lady removed perplexity in minds of the neighbours. He called the young man that worked in her house and said:

"You light the pyre of your father."

The young man lit pyre of his father.

26. IN BECOMING GREAT

The son of a great man could not become great in his life. He asked his father to make him great on a number of occasions. But his father did nothing to make him great. The son felt strongly that his father did not help him become great and developed a strong grouse against him. He openly expressed his feelings before his father. His father coolly heard him and remained silent with no reaction.

The son felt for sure that his father would not make him great. He decided to approach friends of his father to make him great. He met many friends of his father and requested them to make him great. But none helped him out. The son was crestfallen.

One day, at dusk fall, the son went to riverside for an evening walk. He met an elderly man, an old friend of his father, strolling by the riverside. The elderly man greeted the young man and inquired how he was. The young man said with anguish that he wanted to become great, but neither his father nor his influential friends helped him become great. The elderly man said:

"If you want to become great, become great. Why do you depend on others to make you great?"

"How can I become great, unless someone makes me great?" said the young man.

"Young man, what we must realize is none in this world can make any other man great. If someone wants to become great, there is only one person that can make him great. And that one person is none other than he, himself," said the elderly man.

"I don't agree with you. There are many great people, who have become great by virtue of support from their parents," said the young man.

"Your notion is wrong. If someone in this world has become great, it is only by dint of his hard work. Elders can only create opportunities for youngsters to become great. But they cannot make the youngsters great," said the elderly man.

"I think there is only one way out for me to become great," said the young man.

"What is it?" said the elderly man.

"To pray to god to make me great," said the young man.

"Even the god cannot make you great," said the elderly man.

"How do you say so?" said the young man.

"Because I am god," said the elderly man.

Before the stunned son tried to see the god more closely, the god disappeared from his sight.

27. RESPECT FOR FOUNDER

There stood on a pedestal the marble statue of founder of a factory, near main gate of the factory. Every now and then, old retired employees of the factory came to offer floral tributes to the founder. They paid respects to the founding father through elaborate ceremonial rituals of worship.

One day, a ripe old man, retired from the factory very long ago, alighted from a public bus, went to the statue installed on a pedestal and performed a ceremonial ritual, as if in a place of worship. He perambulated around the statue thrice, lighted an oil lamp, broke a coconut, peeled a banana and put it on the pedestal, burnt incense sticks, lighted camphor, put a dot of vermilion on forehead of the statue, garlanded the statue, stood still before the statue with folded hands and offered his respectful prayers to the founder. His family members followed suit.

General Manager of the factory, who happened to pass by the gate, saw the ritual going on near the statue, stopped his car, got down, went to the old man and said to him:

"Who are you?"

"I am one of the former employees of this factory," said the old man.

"What brings you here?" said the General Manager.

"I am celebrating birth day of my great grandson," said the old man.

"That is what is to be performed in a temple," said the General Manager.

"I am celebrating the function only in a temple," said the old man.

"What do you mean?" said the General Manager.

"I mean, sir, this factory is my temple and the statue that I am offering prayers to is deity in the temple," said the old man, with a quiver in his tone.

The General Manager was new to the factory. He said no more. He went to his office and enquired. He came to know that many retired employees of the factory came customarily to statue of the founder and offered their respects ceremonially, on every happy occasion in their families. He was moved.

The General Manager broached the subject before his higher ups and proposed for construction of a temple for the founding father. The higher ups agreed. The higher Management constructed a cute temple amidst a well laid out garden and made provision for working and retired employees of the factory to offer prayers to the deity inside the temple.

28. HERO OF A LADY

In the medieval past, there existed system of courtesans in a kingdom. The courtesans practised their profession publicly under licence from royal authorities. As was the practice in vogue in those days, any one that wanted entertainment from a courtesan was required to pay fee as demanded by the courtesan.

One night, the young son of a noble went to a famous courtesan and desired her company. The courtesan refused. The young man offered to part with any amount that the courtesan demanded. But the courtesan refused to entertain her guest. The young man was enraged. He picked up an argument with the courtesan. The courtesan got wild. She slapped the young man and ordered him to get out of her sight. The young man took the matter very seriously. He went and complained to royal authorities about atrocious behaviour of the courtesan. The royal authorities took the matter seriously, arrested the courtesan and produced her before king in court hall. The king heard the case presented by the case presenter and said to the courtesan:

"Did you slap your guest?"

"I did it," said the courtesan.

"Why did you do it?" said the king.

"I did not like to entertain the guest," said the courtesan.

"Did he not agree to pay what you demanded?" said the king.

"He agreed," said the courtesan.

"What made you refuse the guest and slap him?" said the king.

"I cannot reveal the reason," said the courtesan.

"You must reveal the reason. Otherwise apologise to your guest and oblige his request," said the king.

"I shall not do it," said the courtesan.

"If it is so, you will have to undergo severe punishment," said the king.

"I am prepared to be punished," said the courtesan.

"Do you know what the punishment is?" said the king.

"It does not concern me even if it is death," said the courtesan.

"If you are going against ethos of your profession and prepared for any punishment, there must be some solid reason behind your stout refusal. Tell me whether there is reason or not," said the king.

"There is a reason," said the courtesan.

"What is it?" said the king.

"I fed the young man from my breast, when he was months old," said the courtesan.

The king said no more. He was moved. He said to the courtesan:

"I set you free. You have overwhelmed me with nobility of your action. Ask if you want anything from me."

"Allow me to leave the profession that I am in," said the courtesan.

The king granted desire of the courtesan. He made provision for her to start a new life that she wished for.

29. THE CUE

A young officer, in the service of a king, went on posting, to join as a public servant in a big town. He got rousing welcome from nobles, notables and influential people in the town. A select committee comprising of highly powerful people of the town received the officer with utmost respect. Members of the committee introduced themselves, told the officer about state of affairs in the town, promised all possible help and cooperation in discharge of his duties and made the officer highly comfortable. The officer was immensely happy. He was flattened. He took charge, in his place of work.

A year passed. One day, when he was in his office, messenger in his office reported to him that an aged person wanted to see him. The officer gave his nod. The aged person entered his office, greeted him and occupied a seat offered by the officer. He said:

"I came to tell you something."

"What is it?" said the officer.

"There are some people in this town, who are very good," said the aged person.

"I know it," said the officer.

"They know how to treat an officer well. They please him with pleasantries. They praise him with sweet words. They gratify him with gifts. They accord high class treatment to him in all private and public gatherings. They serve him with high degree of subservience," said the aged person.

"How do you know all this?" said the officer.

"I learnt it out of my experience," said the aged person.

"Who are you?" said the officer.

"An officer in your place in the past," said the aged person.

The officer involuntarily got up from his seat, went to his senior, out of respect, and shook hands with him. He said:

"You have accurately described what is happening in my case." said the officer.

"I have narrated what happened to me with a view that what happened to me should not happen to you," said the aged person.

"What happened to you?" said the officer.

"The people accorded to me highest respect, when I was in office. They overpowered me with closeness of their personal contacts. They showered on me enticing words of flattery, riches and whatever I asked for. They meticulously catered to all my needs. I got swayed. I forgot about my duty. I swerved from discharging my duties independently. I played to tunes of the people, who formed into a close knit coterie, stood around me and cast spell on me. The charm was so powerful that it never occurred to me that I became an agent of action in their hands. Once I remitted office, the people sidelined me from their lives and left me by roadside, uncared for. I was relegated to being a man of no identity. Protect yourself. If you come under influence of these people, you will fail in your designated duty to discharge your duties," said the aged person.

The senior went away. He left behind sufficient stuff for his junior to feed on. The officer pondered over his predicament, realized that there was truth in what the senior said, wriggled out of a binding situation that he was caught in and set himself right. He kept people that connived to fail him in his duty, at bay, and discharged his duties carefully. He did not forget to bow in gratitude to his senior, who saved him from losing his identity.

30. NO HUMANS

Once, a severe famine struck a forest. Water bodies in the forest dried up. Trees withered. Greenery vanished. Herbivorous animals, for want of grass and vegetation, famished and perished. Carnivorous animals, for want of prey animals, pined away. King of the forest, a tiger, saw helplessly plight of the animals languishing in front of his eyes and decided to do something. He convened a meeting and called upon the participants to give their views on how to tide over the situation. Jackal, a wise animal in the gathering, advised the king to take help from a saint that dwelt in the forest. The king agreed. He, accompanied by the jackal and some of his trusted lieutenants, went to see the saint that was in deep penance in a cave on a hillside. He waited until the saint opened his eyes and saw him. The saint said to the tiger:

"What brings you here, king of the forest?"

"I came for your help," said the tiger.

"Tell me what I can do for you," said the saint.

"A famine struck the forest where we are. We are starving of food. Many of beasts in the forest died for lack of food. I am not able to decide how to save my subjects from effect of this famine. Please show us a way out to save ourselves," said the tiger.

"Leave the forest where you are and move to a neighbouring forest, where there is greenery," said the tiger.

"That we cannot do," said the tiger.

"Why?" said the tiger.

"The neighbouring forest is not in our kingdom. It is in the kingdom ruled by a different king," said the tiger.

"Don't talk like humans. Talk like animals. You are not bounded by boundaries," said the tiger.

The tiger and his followers bowed low to the saint and left the place. Same day, they left the forest in which they were and moved out into a neighbouring forest, full of greenery.

31. PLANTS OF ALL

Two neighbours lived side by side in a residential colony. Both were good friends. They had taste for growing plants. They bought many types of plants and planted them in open yards of their houses. The plants grew thick and tall and plants in one house spread out to neighbouring house. The neighbours looked after the plants with high care.

Over the years, for some petty reasons, strains developed in relations of the neighbours. The neighbours stopped talking to each other or seeing each other, eye to eye.

One of the neighbours was highly spiteful. She did something or other to irritate the second neighbour. But the second neighbour was on her guard. She took care not to get drawn into any argument with the first neighbour. Howsoever the first neighbour provoked, the second neighbour learnt to remain calm and quiet. This only added to infuriate the first neighbour further.

First neighbour could not digest coolness of the second neighbour. She got angry. One day, she brought acid and poured on the plants of her neighbour. The poor plants in the neighbouring house, under effect of the acid, burnt and died. The second neighbour felt very sad at what happened. She shed tears out of agony. But she did nothing to fight with her cruel neighbour.

The second neighbour did not react for the gory incident. But her daughter got wild. She picked up an argument with her mother. She said:

"Your neighbour has poured acid and killed our plants. I don't know how you are able to keep quiet?"

"What shall I do?" said the second neighbour.

"She killed our plants. Let us kill her plants," said the daughter.

"I shall never do it?" said the second neighbour.

"Why do you say so?" said the daughter.

"There is nothing like our plants and their plants. All plants are our plants only," said the second neighbour.

32. STRANGE WISH

Once, a disturbing situation arose in a forest. Man mercilessly killed birds and animals in the area. He cut trees indiscriminately. The lush green forest, which teemed with life once upon a time, turned into a barren land, bereft of plants and devoid of living creatures. Birds and animals, which were on their way out of existence, met sadly near foot of a hill, and deliberated upon how to put a stop to mindless destruction brought down upon them. A lead animal in the gathering addressed the creatures that gathered there and solicited their opinion on the subject. Every one expressed that there was immediate need for action to counteract action of the man. But none had any clear cut solution. After a long spell of silence, a little bird tweeted:

"Why we should not request god to save us?"

All in the gathering appreciated the little bird for its suggestion. The leader praised the bird for its participatory spirit and said to it:

"Your idea is very good. If all of you permit me, in behalf of all lining creatures in the forest, I shall pray to god to save us from extinction."

All creatures in the gathering thanked the lead animal for its voluntary offer to pray to god and felicitated the little bird for its groundbreaking tweet. The lead animal took leave of the creatures in the gathering and retired to a solitary spot to sit in penance. It sat in penance in propitiation of god and pleased god with its prayers. The god appeared before the lead animal and said:

"I am pleased with your prayers. Tell me what you want."

"Put good sense in man to save us from destruction," said the lead animal.

"You could have asked me straight to save you from destruction. Why did you ask me to put good sense in man to save you," said the god.

"You may save us at the behest of our request for the present. But as long as man is there with thought to cause destruction to us, there is no permanent safety for us. If you change mindset of man, it is more than your saving us from extinction," said the lead animal.

God appreciated presence of mind of the lead animal and went away to change mindset of man.

33. JOY OF WORKING

Every day, an aged woman collected lunch and other needs for a working day from her home, assorted them in a cane basket, put the basket on her head and left to her field, a little distance away from her home, right in the morning. She reached the field, lowered the basket underneath a tree, and got down to work in the field. Workers worked in her field. But the aged woman chose not to sit idle. She joined the workers and worked along with them. She did myriad jobs that her body co-operated to do. She plucked weeds from among the plants. She walked through the field and checked whether water reached all the plants or not. She helped workers in their works. She sang songs. She encouraged the workers to join her in singing folk songs that uplifted their spirits. She spoke to the workers to know about how they and their family members fared. She resolved disputes that arose between married couples among the workers. She sat with the workers, shared curries with them that she brought from home and took her lunch leisurely. She scared stray animals or birds that came into neighbourhood of the field. She soulfully greeted acquaintances that happened to walk by the field. She played pranks with young womenfolk. She electrified the surroundings with her presence. She remained most conspicuous either by her presence or absence in her place of work.

One day, owner of a neighbouring farm land greeted the aged woman, enquired after her health and said:

"You have your sons and grandsons and other women in your family. Why do you take the trouble of coming to the field every day and working from dawn to dusk?"

"My family members are very busy," said the woman.

"How are they busy at home?" said the farmer.

"They enjoy watching television, chatting, eating and passing time in merriment," said the woman.

"You too can fall in line with them and enjoy," said the woman.

"I cannot do it," said the woman.

"Why?" said the woman.

"I enjoy working," said the woman.

34. THE TALLEST SPIRE

Residents in a wealthy residential colony felt the need for a place of worship in their colony. They assembled, discussed and decided to construct a temple in the colony. They deliberated upon which god they were to erect a shrine for. They could not narrow down to any single god. They took a decision to build five shrines in the name of five different gods in different parts of the colony and built the same.

In a slum, in close proximity of the colony, many poor people lived. They too wanted to have a place of worship in centre of their slum. They discussed among themselves and decided upon the god, in the name of whom, the shrine was to be erected. They were not rich. They could not raise funds for construction of the shrine immediately. They made a rule. As per the rule, every earner in the slum set aside a small portion of his earning towards fund for construction of the shrine. Everyone in the slum stuck to the rule meticulously. Over the years, the fund grew large enough. A committee named for construction of the shrine used the fund and started building a shrine in the slum. The construction, for paucity of funds, progressed at snail's pace and continued for many years, gradually and continuously. And finally, after more than a decade, it took shape that was simply striking. A shrine for a god worshipped by the slum dwellers came gorgeously up, with a sky scraping tower that stood imposingly tall. Tower of the shrine stood tallest among towers of other shrines that came into existence in the entire neighbourhood.

35. SUCCESSOR

A visionary founded a factory that manufactured an engineering product. Over a period of time, he developed the factory into a huge set up that forayed into manufacturing many types of products. He became old. He felt it was time for him to retire from service. He wanted to hand over the factory to his successor. He opened out what was there in his mind to some of his confidants.

The founder had a son. The son was educated. Everyone in the factory looked forward for the son to take over position of his father.

Finally a day came, when the successor was to take reins from the founder. The founder called for a high level meeting of all that mattered most in transfer of his role and addressed them:

"As you know, I have called for this meeting to name a successor for the factory after me. Before I name the successor, I would like to share my heartfelt feelings with you.

Firstly, I thank one and all of you for the great support you gave me right from inception of this factory until now. If the factory is what it is today, it is all because of you and your concerted efforts.

I have headed the factory, as long as I could do it. But with age advanced, I am of the opinion that I must step down and hand over the factory to my successor. On this occasion, I appeal fervently to all of you to extend support to the successor as much as you had extended to me in the past. I am sure, with support of all of you, the successor will take the factory to new heights."

Invitees in the assembly maintained pin drop silence. They eagerly awaited formal announcement of name of the successor. Everyone looked at son of the founder, who sat in front row in the hall. At last, the founder made the announcement. Everyone in the assembly was dismayed. The founder did not name his son successor, but someone else. Someone from the assembly raised the issue:

"Why did you name someone other than your own son successor of the factory?"

"I know that my son can run the factory successfully after me. But I do not want someone, who can simply run the factory successfully after me. I want someone, who can catapult the factory to far reaching heights. I have chosen a successor, who can do it and my son will work under him, until he graduates to become a successor in future," said the founder.

The attendees in the conference hall heartily hailed decision of the founding father and welcomed his decision with nonstop claps that reverberated in the hall.

36. DIVERSION OF MIND

A house holder faced a strange situation at his home front. His mother and wife developed differences over some or other petty issue, very frequently, got into argument and fell out with each other. When the warring parties brought the matter for mediation before him, he heard them patiently, talked to them coolly, took care not to side with anyone and resolved the issue amicably, without hurting sentiments of anyone. When the episode repeated again and again, he was worried. He counselled both the parties separately and collectively and tried to put in them good sense to learn to live together and not to lose their tempers. But his advice did not yield desired results.

The householder often lost peace of mind on account of frequent quarrels between his mother and wife. He was highly disturbed. He discussed the problem with some of his close friends and sought their suggestion. But he got the stunning feedback that quarrels between mother-in-law and daughter-in-law were very common in every household and they were not to be taken seriously. But the householder was not convinced. He thought that he could not live with the problem persisting in his family. He wanted to find a permanent solution for the problem. He analysed situations that culminated in quarrels between his mother and wife. He realized that quarrels precipitated, mainly because his mother tried to interfere in works of his wife and his wife did not like the interference. He wanted to tell his mother straight not to meddle in affairs of his wife. But he did not do it, because he did not want to offend his mother. He thought and found a way out. One day, he called his mother and said:

"You are a good narrator of stories. Why don't you tell me a story every night?"

"I have already narrated all stories that I know. I don't have new stories to narrate," said the mother.

"Learn new stories," said the householder.

"Wherefrom shall I learn?" said the mother.

"Read books to get to know about new stories," said the householder.

"How can I read books? I am not literate," said the mother.

"Learn to read," said the householder.

"Teach me. I shall do it," said the mother.

The householder requested his wife to teach his mother how to write and read basic alphabet of his mother tongue and she agreed. Mother of the householder liked studies and she studied under guidance of her daughter-in-law. She applied herself seriously to learning and, very soon, she started reading story books meant for school children. She enjoyed reading. She remained immersed in studies from morning to night. She hardly found time to watch what his daughter-in-law turned teacher did. She minded her business and the daughter-in-law minded her business. Scope for interference between the erstwhile war heads vanished. Permanent peace settled in the household. The householder enjoyed bliss of peace.

37. SON OF A SCHOLAR

The son of a scholar was not a happy man. The reason for his unhappiness was very queer. He was not called by his christened name. He was only referred to as son of his father, who was a great scholar. He was highly anguished.

He did not know how to be called by his own name rather than being called son of his father.

One day, he went to a friend of his father to vent out the anguish in him. But he could not open out what was there in his mind, straightaway. He hesitated and stood silently before him. The friend of his father said:

"What brings you here, my son?"

"I came on a purpose," said son of the scholar.

"What is it?" said friend of the scholar.

"I am finding it very delicate to tell you," said son of the scholar.

"Please tell me without hesitation," said friend of the scholar.

"Everyone is addressing me as son of my father. Nobody is calling me by my name," said son of the scholar.

"I know it happens with everyone, who is the son of a great man," said friend of the scholar.

"Is there no way out for this?" said son of the scholar.

"There is," said friend of the scholar.

"What is it?" said son of the scholar.

"Become greater than your father," said friend of the scholar.

"What will happen by it?" said son of the scholar.

"People will call you by your name and your father will be referred to as father of you," said friend of the scholar.

The son made up his mind to become greater than his father.

38. SHORTCUT

An educational counsellor went on a tour from school to school and spoke on how to study and how to do well in examinations. He mastered the subject and told students the process of carrying out studies systematically and in well sequenced steps. Both students as well as teachers in schools appreciated his speech.

One day, the counsellor went to a school and delivered his speech in assembly hall, before a large gathering of students and faculty members. At end of the speech, he offered to answer questions raised by the attendees. One student stood up and said:

"Sir, I appreciate, you have elucidated in your informative speech how to study and do well in examinations."

"Thank you," said the counsellor.

"But what you have said is not new to us. We know very well about it," said the student.

"If you know what I have said, it is very nice. Please follow it and try to do well in examinations," said the counsellor.

"Is there no shortcut for elaborate study to do well in examinations?" said the student.

"There is no shortcut," said the counsellor.

"I am looking out for a one," said the student.

"I too did the same, when I was of your age," said the counsellor.

"Please tell in detail what is your experience about it," said the student.

"I researched for a shortcut way for how to do well in examinations without studying hard, until I realized that there was no shortcut for elaborate study. By the time the realization dawned upon me, I became too old to write examinations," said the counsellor.

"What ultimately did you do?" said the student.

"I turned into an educational counsellor," said the counsellor.

"What for?" said the student.

"To tell students that there is not shortcut for studying well and to do well in examinations," said the counsellor.

39. OUTSOURCING

A king was a pleasure hunter. He considered ruling as a big botheration. He often felt how good it could be, if there was someone who did his job, and he revelled in pleasures happily with no interruption. He expressed the same to his chief minister. The chief minister was a wise man. He advised the king to refrain from such thoughts. But the king was very persistent. He told the chief minister to look out for a courtier, who could discharge duties of a king in his name. The chief minister obliged and named a courtier. The king entrusted responsibility of ruling to the courtier and devoted his time to running after pleasures.

The courtier discharged duties of the king very effectively. He made available all conceivable pleasures at disposal of the king to revel in. The king enjoyed pleasures. The courtier enjoyed power.

One fine morning, the courtier declared himself new king of the kingdom.

40. IDEATION

The son of a scholar was a writer. He had deep urge to write. He showed no interest in household works and remained immersed in only writing. The scholar understood taste of his son and remained calm, even if he did no household works. One day, the writer said to his father:

"Father, I have a problem. Can you find a solution for it?"

"What is it?" said the scholar.

"I have deep passion for writing. I feel like spending all my time only in writing. But, for some reason, when I sit to write, I am not able to write," said the writer.

"Why are you not able to write, when you sit to write?" said the scholar.

"Ideas in my mind dry up. My mind becomes blank. However hard I try to find ideas, my mind fails to get at them," said the writer.

"Do one thing," said the scholar.

"What is it?" said the writer.

"Stop writing and start working. From today onwards, go to our field and take up cultivation," said the scholar.

"Why?" said the writer.

"You are not fit for writing," said the scholar.

The son was stunned. He was pained. He could not decide how to react to disparaging words of his father. He hurled scornful looks at his father, hurried away from home and went to his field to join a team of labourers that raised a crop in his field. He decided to give up writing and get into farming. True to his resolution, he dedicated himself to growing crops in his field, with no other avocation.

Within a few months, the son became a successful farmer. In addition, he became a published author of his works. He went to his father and said haughtily:

"I have become a published author." said the writer.

"I heartily congratulate you," said the scholar.

"You said I am unfit for writing," said the writer.

"I made you fit for writing, by sending you to the field work," said the scholar.

"What do you mean?" said the writer.

"If we sit at home and try to generate ideas, we can't generate them. But if we get into doing physical works, ideas start coming to us in continuous streams. For you to get ideas, I made you get engaged in physical activity in the form of farm work," said the scholar.

The son fell prostrate at feet of his father and sought his pardon for evil thoughts that he cradled against him in his mind. The father lifted his son, took him into his embrace and kissed him.

41. DOWNFALL

A boy in his late teens swerved from righteous path. He got into evil company. He took to bad habits. He did many things that he was not supposed to do. His father sensed the situation. One day, he called his son into his room and said to him:

"You are on wrong track."

"Don't worry. I am not," said the son.

"I am cautioning you, because it is my responsibly to caution you," said the father.

"Thank you for your advice. Be assured that I am not on wrong track," said the son.

"Remember one thing. Bad habits start in a small way and multiply in a big way. They grow very fast by unseen degrees. They are cancerous. If you don't nip them in the bud, you can't cure them at a later stage. Take my advice. Distance yourself from evil company of your friends and correct yourself," said the father.

"Call me anything. Don't call my friends bad. They are good," said the son.

"I am advising you, because I am here today before you. I shall not be able to advise you tomorrow, because, even if you want, I shall not be there by then," said the father.

The son took words of his father lightly and went away from there. The father did no more bother to give advices.

A day came, when the son was in deep trouble. He looked out for someone, who could rescue him from the abyss, into which he fell. But he found none, who could help him. His father, who could retrieve him from trouble, left for heavenly abode, long ago.

42. HUMILIATION

Municipal administration of a town conducted competitions for school children. The competitions included sports, literary and cultural activities. All schools in the town participated in the competitions. Management of every school selected best of their students for each event of competition, put them under a trainer and sent them for the competitions. Students from every school proved their mettle in one or other competition and bore away prizes, excepting students from one school, who got no prize. Schools that bagged prizes jeered at the school that failed to secure any prize. Head master of the school that got no prize got humiliated. He turned very sad. He took defeat of his students as his own defeat, took it to heart, fell sick and absented from going to school.

Some students of the school came to know that people from other schools laughed at their school and their head master got humiliated. They got furious. They went to see the head master at his residence and said to him:

"Please tell us who has humiliated our school. We shall not leave them. We shall take revenge."

"What will you do?" said the head master.

"We shall give them a taste of our physical reaction for their banter," said the students.

"I don't want you to do it," said the head master.

"Please advise what else we shall do," said the head master.

"Make sure that our students will stand first in all events in the next round of competitions," said the head master.

The students agreed. They prepared very hard for the next round of competitions, proved their mettle and avenged the humiliation caused to their head master.

43. CASE WORKER

There was a case worker in the service of a king. He was responsible to hear grievances brought to his notice by both people in service of the king as well as general public, prepare a case and present it to higher ups for resolution. He was very effective in his role play. He became old and retired from service. The king asked his chief minister to select a good candidate and put him in place of the retired case worker. The chief minister took up the job.

When the chief minister took quite some time to appoint a new case worker, the king got jittery and questioned the chief minister for the inordinate delay. The chief minister explained:

"I am on the job. Very soon, I shall do it."

"Case worker is the lowest in echelon of the grievance redressal system. Why are you taking very long time to select a proper case worker to take the place of the retiree?" said the king.

"I am looking out for a proper candidate," said the chief minister.

"What is so great about the selection?" said the king.

"Selection of a case worker is very crucial," said the chief minister.

"How?" questioned the king.

"Final judgement in a case depends largely on how the case is perceived and presented by the case worker," said the chief minister.

"How do you say so?" said the king.

"A case worker, while preparing a case, puts together all facts and figures of the case and presents the case to his higher ups, in a way that he understands. He is the first judge that gives his opinion about the case. Mostly, people in higher rung of judgement go by opinion of the case worker and they tend to be influenced by what the case worker conveys. If there is subjectivity in opinion expressed by the case worker, outcome of the final judgment is likely to go awry. That is why I am looking out for a candidate, who is wise, honest, objective and is endowed with good presentation skill," said the chief minister.

The king appreciated criteria fixed by the chief minister for selection of the case worker and gave him free hand in the selection. The chief minister selected a good case worker, very soon.

44. I AM MANAGEMENT

An act of insubordination by a workman in a department attracted mild punishment from the departmental head. The incident led to labour unrest in the department. All workmen got together and threatened to strike work. The departmental head cautioned them from resorting to such an act. But the workmen were in no mood to heed. They sat in their seats and struck work. The departmental head counselled the workmen to call off the strike. But the workmen stuck to their stand. After persuasion by some union leaders, the workmen called off strike and attended to their duties.

But the departmental head did not take stance of the workmen kindly. He advised for deduction of wages for strike period as per standing orders of the factory. Wages of the workmen were deducted. The workmen got highly furious. They burst into chamber of the departmental head and called him names and hurled threats. The departmental head remained unshaken. He listened coolly to what his workmen said. After a few hours, the workmen got weary and left the chamber. Senior union representatives met the departmental head and said:

"Please repeal the action."

"I have taken action not to repeal it," said the departmental head.

"What you have done is wrong," said the union representatives.

"Don't ratify my work," said the departmental head.

"If you think coolly you will understand that what you have done is wrong," said the union representatives.

"I thought coolly and took action. I did nothing wrong. Had I not taken action, I would have failed in my duty and erred," said the departmental head.

"If you don't retract your stand, we shall have to report the matter to management," said the union representatives

"Who is management? I am management. Know it and talk," shouted the departmental head.

The union leaders had no more to say. They moved out of the cabin. Workmen of the department, who waited outside, met the union leaders and asked what happened. A leader remarked:

"I feel like saluting your boss."

"What happened. Did he agree to repeal the action?" said a workman.

"He did not repeal action," said the union leader.

"If it is so, why do you feel like saluting the departmental head?" said a workman.

"Whenever we meet an executive in this factory to represent a problem and request him to solve it, invariably, he, however high placed is he, says that he is helpless, he cannot take a decision on his own and he will have to consult his higher ups before committing to do it. Going by nature of management in this factory, we really wonder who part of management is and who not part of management in this factory is. For the first time, we have come across an executive who authoritatively says 'I am management'. Hats off to him," said the union leader.

45. WILL OF GOD

An old man was at brink of his life. He lost his wife. His children stayed away from him. He lived all alone. He was highly desolate. He was at a loss to understand what for he lived. Every day, he went to a temple and prayed to god to take him away early.

One evening, the old man went to the temple, at the time of twilight. The priest in temple lighted lamps. Birds perched in niches of tall tower of the temple chirped. The old man offered prayers to god, retired to a corner, leaned against a pillar and sat calmly, drowned deeply in solitary reflection of his past. The priest observed the old man and greeted him:

"You are not your usual self these days."

"You are right," said the old man.

"What is the reason?" said the priest.

"My wife passed away," said the old man.

"That is very sad," said the priest.

"My sons are staying away from me," said the old man.

"It is painful," said the priest.

"All my acquaintances have left the world long ago," said the old man.

"I know," said the priest.

"With none with me, I am feeling lonely and deserted. I am praying to god to take me away at the earliest," said the old man.

"Don't pray," said the priest.

"Why?" said the old man.

"God will not take you," said the priest.

"Why?" said the old man.

"God wants you to do something important before you go," said the priest.

"How do you say so?" said the old man.

"If the god has taken one and all from you and has left only you behind, please understand that he is expecting something great to be done by you before you leave the world," said the priest.

"Is it?" said the old man.

"Yes," said the priest.

The old man did not pray any more to god to take him away early.

46. ETHICS

An hotelier ran a restaurant in a busy city centre. He had roaring business. Customers from all over the city and from neighbouring places thronged to the restaurant, right from predawn to late into night. The hotelier ran the hotel very well, with total dedication. He took extreme care to satisfy his customers. He inspected quality of items used in preparation of dishes and ensured that the food served to guests was of high class quality. He delighted customers with overwhelming hospitality and taste of food that tickled taste buds of customers.

He started the hotel as a start-up, when he was in beginning of his earning career. He started it in a small way, in a tiled bungalow. Over the years, he ploughed back good part of the money earned out of the business in further improvement of the business and erected a good building in place of the erstwhile tiled bungalow. Going by volume of business, he could have minted money out of the business. But he was not greedy. He was satisfied with what he earned. More than amassing wealth, he concentrated on satisfying customers.

On one or more occasions, suppliers of low quality items required for preparation of food items, offered to make supplies at very cheap rate. But the hotelier was on his guard. He did not buy the low quality items. He preferred satisfying his customers to reducing quality of the food items. He ran his business successfully and satisfactorily for more than fifty years and finally handed over the business to his only son.

Son of the businessman was wholly unhappy with way of business of his father. He felt that his father, even after being in business for more than fifty years, did not become rich. He decided to shift his focus to becoming rich. He left to winds ethics followed by his father and started using inferior quality items for food preparation. Image of the hotel built by his father sustained the hotel business for some time. Later on, it suffered. Customers that patronised the hotel for more than a half century moved away from it. The hotel went out of business and closed down.

47. BARREN LAND

A farmer had a piece of barren land. He worked very hard to grow crops in it. He ploughed, watered, planted seeds, put fertilizers, sprayed germicides and tended the plants carefully in the land. But the land had a problem. Weeds in large numbers grew in the land alongside crops. The farmer took pains to remove the weeds from time to time and protect the crop.

A second farmer, who had a piece of land beside land of the first farmer, saw the first farmer and ridiculed:

"Why are you wasting your efforts on raising crop in the land?"

"Why do you say that I am wasting my effort?" said the first farmer.

"Soil of fields in this area is not good. Weeds come up fast in midst of crops. Removing them is a big botheration. That is the reason why, I stopped cultivating my land," said the second farmer.

"Notwithstanding it, I want to cultivate crop in my land," said the first farmer.

"What for?" said the second farmer

"If I raise crop, crop will come up and alongside some weeds too will come up. If I don't raise crop, crop will not come up and only weeds will come up. I do not want to leave my field exclusively for weeds to grow," said the first farmer.

The second farmer fathomed what the first farmer hinted at. He decided at once to grow a crop in his field too.

48. IRRITABLE CHARACTER

A young man got into a train and occupied the berth reserved for him. The train started. A middle aged co-passenger, who sat beside the passenger, greeted him:

"Where are you going up to?"

"Up to the last station the train is going to," said the young man.

"What are you doing there?" said the middle aged man.

"I am employed in a Company there," said the young man.

"How come, you have come here?" said the middle aged man.

"It is my native place," said the young man.

"Are your family members here?" said the middle aged man.

"All my family members are with me, where I am staying," said the young man.

"Then what made you come here?" said the middle aged man.

"My relatives are here," said the young man.

"Who are your relatives? Tell me their names. I may know some of them," said the middle aged man.

The young man told some names. The middle aged man heard them and said:

"I have not heard about any one of the names that you said."

"What shall I do, if you have not heard about the names," said the young man at the verge of losing patience.

"I want to check whether you are speaking truth or lie," said the middle aged man.

"Shut up," shouted the young man.

"How dare do you say 'shut up'?" said the middle aged man, turning serious.

"If you utter one more word, I don't know what I shall do," razed the young man.

"What will you do?" said the middle aged man, braving the young man.

"See what I can do," raved the young man and put a hard slap on cheek of the middle aged man.

The young man feared reaction from other passengers in the compartment. But no one uttered even a single word. Instead, the co-passengers looked at the young man appreciatively. The middle aged man, jeered at by other passengers in the compartment, lowered his head in shame, collected his luggage and moved away from the place to another compartment, with down cast eyes. After his exit, passengers in the compartment shook hands with the young man and congratulated him. The young man was surprised. He exclaimed:

"Why are you congratulating me?"

"You have done what we could not do," said the co-passengers.

"What do you mean?" said the young man.

"He irritated us as much as he irritated you, before you came here," said the co-passengers.

The young man was in a mood of repentance for his rash action. But after hearing the co-passengers, he felt that there was no need for him to repent.

49. SORCERER

A sorcerer stayed with his wife and son, in a hut in suburbs of a hillside tribal village. He performed a ritual to know about what ailment a person got and how to cure him of it. With help of the ritual, he cured many patients that came to him with unknown ailments, from far and near. He inherited the practice from his father and forefather. He lived on whatever little he earned out of the practice. He established for himself the name of a good curing hand in the entire neighbourhood.

Wife of the sorcerer was a very simple and naive lady. She had very high respect for her husband. She watched with curiosity how her husband performed rituals and cured patients of their ailments.

One afternoon, a middle aged couple brought their young son with the complaint that the boy suffered from some unknown ailment and he lost his weight. The sorcerer heard them, assured them of his help and made them sit in front yard of the hut. He hurriedly went underneath a neem tree in a corner of the front yard, swept a place with broomstick, sprayed on it water mixed with cow dung, made some floral designs with chalk powder on the place, put a wide topped bowl in midst of the place, poured water mixed with turmeric and vermilion in it and asked the boy to come near and show his face in water in the bowl. The boy showed his face in coloured water of the bowl and went back to his seat. The sorcerer bent over the bowl and saw keenly into the water. After a minute, he raised his head, smiled, approached the boy and said:

"By chance, did you go to any desolate place in the last few days?"

"I did," said the boy.

"Where did you go?" said the sorcerer.

"When I took out my cattle for grazing, I happened to stray into a deserted place that was frighteningly eerie," said the boy.

"There started the problem. You came under overpowering effect of an evil spirit staying there. Don't worry. I shall perform an antidote to make the spirit run away from you. Go home with your parents. You will become normal in a couple of days," said the sorcerer.

The boy and his parents paid their respects to the sorcerer and departed. Wife of the sorcerer, who watched the ritual closely and keenly said to her husband:

"What did you see in coloured water of the bowl?"

"The cause of ailment of the boy," said the sorcerer.

"I want to ask you something, if you don't mind," said the sorcerer's wife.

"Ask," said the sorcerer.

"When you are able to see everything on face of earth through the ritual that you are performing, why don't you see something for us?" said the sorcerer's wife.

"What shall I see?" said the sorcerer.

"Hidden treasures that can make us rich," said the sorcerer's wife.

"I cannot do it," said the sorcerer.

"Why?" said the sorcerer's wife.

"We can see what is helpful to others. We are forbidden from seeing what is useful to us," said the sorcerer.

"What happens, if we see for what we want?" said the sorcerer's wife.

"I shall lose my power of divinity," said the sorcerer.

"How do you say so?" said the sorcerer's wife.

"According to the originator, who started this practice, anyone that misuses this divine skill for his selfish end is destined to lose his power of divinity," said the sorcerer.

The sorcerer's wife felt very sorry for her husband. She felt that her husband could have unravelled mysteries of hidden treasures save for the condition imposed by the originator. She sadly moved away from there to attend to her household chores. The sorcerer sat alone looking at his innocent wife walking away. He did not want to reveal that he possessed no divine skills and he carried out the rituals only to create belief in customers that he came to know causes of ailments suffered by his patients, through the rituals.

50. RISE AND FALL

A learned speaker delivered a moving speech before a congregation of many invitees in a lecture hall. He spoke on rise and fall in life. At end of the speech, he remarked:

"Supporting a man who is on rise is very easy. But supporting a man who is on fall is very difficult. If you are on the path of rise, you will find somebody, who can support you. But if you are on the path of falling down, you can hardly come across anybody who can support you. Therefore, be always on your guard to be on rise and never be on fall."

"How do you say that supporting a man who is on rise is very easy and supporting a man who is on fall is very difficult?" questioned an invitee from the gathering.

"When a man is on rise, effort to be put in by a supporter to support the man is less, since his effort is total effort for rise minus effort by the riser to rise. Therefore anyone is likely to come forward to support a riser. On the other hand, if a man is on fall, effort to be put in by a supporter to support the man is very high, since effort by the faller is zero and effort by the supporter to prevent the faller from free fall is phenomenally high. Therefore no one is likely to come forward to support a faller," reasoned out the speaker.

The audience was convinced with logic put forward by the speaker.

51. BLESSING

A father, who stayed in a town, took his young son to a village fair held in his native place. The fair was for the local deity. Devotees from within and outside the village thronged to the fair in large numbers. The father and son walked through the crowd. They went to the temple of the local deity, offered their prayers and came out. The father, on way, met some acquaintances of his native village and talked to them. The little boy moved close to his father, watching with awe, scenes peculiar to the fair and various eye catching articles on display for sale in shops all around. He beamed with ecstasy.

Meantime, an elderly lady with a hunched back approached the father and son. She held in her hand a brass plate with a tiny idol of the local deity seated on a heap of vermilion on it. She looked at the father from a close range, recognised him by his name and said:

"How are you?"

"I am doing well," said the father.

"I knew you from the days when you came to the fair along with your father. Now you have become a father and are coming with your son," said the lady.

"Yes, mother," said the father.

"I am very happy to see you after many years. Come, I shall put a dot of vermilion on foreheads of you and your son," said the lady.

The father obliged. The lady put large dots of vermilion on foreheads of both father and son. She said to the son:

"You are a cute boy. What are you doing?"

"I am going to school," said the boy.

"Do it. You are blessed to become great. I reveal this to you at the instance of the village goddess," said the lady.

What the elderly lady said got registered on mind of the boy. The boy believed strongly that the village goddess gave a blessing and the elderly lady conveyed it to him. The belief worked like a tonic. The boy worked hard and translated into reality blessing of the goddess. He became great.

52. PROHIBITION

A king faced a tight pecuniary situation. He was not able to meet both ends of revenue and expenditure. He called for a meeting of his courtiers and solicited their opinion on how to get out of the situation. One of the counsellors said:

"Let us increase revenue by additional levies."

"Levies are already more. I don't think we can increase them further," said the king.

"There is a way out," said the counsellor.

"What is it?" said the king.

"Prohibition of liquor is in place in our kingdom. We can think of lifting prohibition and legalising production and sale of liquor. We can levy heavily on both production and sale of liquor," said the counsellor.

"We have prohibited liquor, keeping in view health of our state subjects. It may be unethical on our part to lift the prohibition," said the king.

"The fact is, even though prohibition is in place, it is not very effective in practice. Many unscrupulous people are brewing liquor illegally and making money out of it. Instead of allowing such people to get going with their illegal activities, it is better for us to legitimize production of liquor and impose levy on it," said the counsellor.

"How much money can we get out of the levy?" said the king.

"So much that it will not only meet deficit in our budget, but also make the budget surplus," said the counsellor.

"Splendid. If that is the case, let us lift prohibition, legalise production and sale of liquor and levy taxes on it," said the king.

Order of the king came into force at once. Legalised liquor got available everywhere throughout the kingdom. People, who took liquor stealthily, hitherto, started taking it publicly and freely with no inhibition. Consumers, very few earlier, increased in numbers manifold. Revenue of the state looked up. The king and his administration were very happy. Deficit budget of the state turned into surplus budget.

Buoyed up with the rise in revenue, the king announced a slew of measures for welfare of his people. He sent emissaries to every village in his kingdom to identify the needy that deserved help and distribute money for them. The emissaries spread out across the kingdom on their designated duty.

One of the emissaries went to a village, identified the poor and needy there, and distributed money to them, one after another. He came across an old lady who flatly refused money from the king. The emissary was surprised. He said:

"You are poor. The king is pleased to help you. Take the money given by the king. It will support your livelihood."

"It is sinful money. I don't want it. Let the king keep it," said the old lady.

"How dare do you criticize our king. You will be punished for your impropriety," said the emissary.

"I am prepared to be punished, if I have uttered anything wrong. Take me to the king, if you want," said the old lady.

The emissary took the old lady to the king. The king, in presence of his courtiers, questioned the lady:

"Why did you call money sent by me sinful?"

"Since you have earned it out of ruining of two bread earners in my family," said the old lady.

"Explain clearly," said the king.

"When prohibition was in place, both my son and grandson worked and earned their bread. After the liquor became available freely everywhere, my son and grandson have become drunkards. They became addicted to drinking. They stopped earning and in turn are bothering womenfolk in the house to supply coppers for their liquor. Earlier men folk in my family worked. Now, courtesy lifting of prohibition, womenfolk are working. Reintroduction of liquor has spoiled two of my family members. In my opinion, you are giving me back a part of the money that you have earned out of spoiling two of my family members. That is why I called it sinful money,"

"Do you know what punishment you will get for your rude talk?" said the king.

"I have not thought of it. If speaking out what is there in my mind is an offence, you may award any punishment that you deem fit. But before punishing me, be pleased to think that there are many women in this kingdom, who have their families ruined due to the liquor menace," said the old lady.

The king got to think. He inquired and found out that there was truth in what the old lady said. He did not like to collect levy that cost lives and livelihood of his people. He did not discuss anymore with anyone. He took an independent decision. He clamped down prohibition again with iron hand. He richly rewarded the old lady that made his eyes open with her fearless feedback. A few in the kingdom cursed the king. But many a one blessed the king.

53. NEW BOSS

An assistant developed a view that his boss did not treat him well. He felt that his boss assigned to him jobs more than what he could do, did not give him recognition for what he did and did not recommend for his accelerated promotions from time to time. He concluded that he worked under a wrong boss and it was time for him to get out him at the earliest. He prepared an application for transfer and submitted it to his boss. The boss said:

"What is the matter?"

"I am not able to work here. I want a transfer," said the subordinate.

"Are you sure you will be able to work elsewhere?" said the boss.

"I think so," said the subordinate.

"Where do you want to go?" said the boss.

"I am prepared to go wherever I am transferred to," said the subordinate.

The boss forwarded the application to HR department and got his assistant transferred the same day. The assistant was surprised with fastness of the transfer. But he was happy. He went to report in the department where he was transferred to. He reported to the new boss, worked with him for a week and understood that his previous boss was many times kind, considerate and accommodative. He cursed himself for his thoughtless act of asking for a transfer to the new boss. He went back to his former boss and requested him to take him back. The former boss agreed. But it took quite some time for the second transfer to materialize. By the time the second transfer materialized, the assistant was wholly changed. He served his first boss with utmost respect and obedience.

54. HONEST MAN

A man was highly honest. He adopted honesty as a way of life. He neither did any dishonest work nor did he tolerate dishonest work from others. He championed the cause of honesty, in all walks of life, at his home front, society as well as work place. He practised honesty both in thought and action. He was a peerless protagonist of honesty.

Because of excessive obsession with honesty, the man faced many problems. He was repulsed at home and feared in society. Many people, who were good friends of him, moved away from him, disgusted with his uncompromising nature. Slowly, the honest man realized that no one liked him in society and many people jeered and jibed at him. He perceived that it became increasingly difficult for him to move in society with his inflexible attitude. Initially he thought that he was on right course and every one would respect him. But when something other than that happened, he realized that there was something wrong with him and it was necessary for him to change, in order for him to continue in society. He went to a good adviser for a piece of advice. The adviser said:

"What is your problem?"

"I am not able to adjust in society," said the honest man.

"Why?" said the adviser.

"I am not able to tolerate dishonesty in society," said the honest man.

"Remove dishonesty from society," said the adviser.

"That I am not able to do," said the honest man.

"Become dishonest," said the adviser.

"I can't even think of it," said the honest man.

"Do one thing. Remain honest. Keep doing what is right in your view. Stop preaching. A day will come when others in society will appreciate what you are doing and they will emulate you sooner or later," said the adviser.

Advice of the adviser appealed to the honest man. He stopped preaching about honesty to others. He remained honest, regardless of what others thought about him. Truly a day came, when people around him recognised his honesty and towed the line of honesty.

55. POSITIVITY

A learned speaker addressed a gathering of many people in assembly hall of a town. People from all walks of life from the town attended to the speech. The speaker spoke on need to weed out negativity from mind. He said;

"Negativity in mind is dangerous. It produces many undesirable elements. It gives rise to envy, hatred, rivalry, revengefulness and everything that is bad and detrimental. It tells upon health. It invades space in mind. It drives out good and virtuous thoughts from mind and occupies space in it, forcibly. It feeds on resourcefulness of a man and siphons off all his energy. Like how a parasitic germ eats away crop in a field and makes the field barren and unfit for growth of crop, negativity pollutes mind.

Never let negativity enter your mind. Keep yourself away from it."

"How to remove negativity from mind?" said a student from audience.

"Weed it out," said the speaker.

"That I am not able to do," said the student.

"Why?" said the speaker.

"I am always filled with thoughts of rivalry against my class mates, who are good at studies and are close to competing with me. However hard I am thinking of throwing thoughts of rivalry from my mind, I am not able to do it," said the student.

"I too have similar experience," said a businessman from the audience.

"What is your problem?" said the speaker.

"At times, I get filled with thoughts of eliminating competitors in the way of my business. Even though I try to convince myself that competition is a way of life, I am not able to throw away such undesirable thoughts from my mind," said the businessman.

"My experience is not different," said a politician.

"Tell me what your problem is," said the speaker.

"My mind is always full of thoughts of causing damage to my rivals in politics and those who are poised against me," said the politician.

When some more people from the audience expressed themselves and told the speaker that in spite of best of their efforts to throw negative thoughts from their minds, they were not able to do so, the speaker said:

"I understand the problems expressed by you. I know that it is impossible to throw negatives thoughts from mind straightaway and keep mind free from them. Even if you try to throw them out forcibly, they come back swarming like flies, as long as mind is empty."

"If that is the case, how to drive out negative thoughts from mind?" said a professional from audience.

"There is a way out for it," said the speaker.

"What is it?" said the professional.

"We need to employ an agent, who acts in behalf of us and drives negative thoughts out of our mind," said the speaker.

"Who is the agent?" said the professional.

"Positivity," said the speaker.

"We don't understand you," said the professional.

"I mean we must employ positivity to drive out the negativity from mind and occupy the position vacated by negativity," said the speaker.

"How does it help?" said the professional.

"Positivity in mind not only drives out negativity from mind, but also does not allow negativity to storm back into mind," said the speaker.

"Will you please elaborate it?" said the professional.

"Concentrate on doing something useful seriously. It works like an agent of positivity and helps drive away negativity from mind," said the speaker.

The audience gave a big applause for what the speaker said.

56. CLIMBING UP A HILL

A boy regularly went up a hill in his village, on which there was a cave shrine. He went to deity in the shrine, offered prayers and enjoyed the hill breeze. He became older, finished his studies, left the village and went away to a far off city for employment. He became old. After retirement from service, he returned to his native village, renovated his ancestral house and settled down in it. He felt very happy to return to his home place after a long time and spend retired life there.

One day, right in the morning, he set out from his home, went to the hill on which the shrine was there and went up to the shrine ecstatically. He felt very happy to offer prayers to the deity after many decades. He spent time in the shrine and on the hilltop until noon, descended the hill and reached back home. He did not inform his wife where he went. His wife was worried. She said:

"Where did you go?"

"I went out," said the husband.

"You didn't even tell me where you went to," said the wife.

"I went to the hillside," said the husband.

"Why did you go there?" said the wife.

"I wanted to see the shrine atop the hill?" said the husband.

"Did you go there?" said the wife.

"Yes," said the husband.

"But how did you go up the hill?" said the wife.

"Why? I climbed steps and went up the hill," said the husband.

"How could you do it? You are suffering from knee pain and you are not able to walk even a few steps," said the wife.

"Yes. What you say is right. But it is a fact that I went up the hill," said the husband.

"How could you do it? The hill is pretty high," said the wife.

"Shall I tell you the truth?" said the husband.

"Tell me," said the wife.

"I completely forgot that I suffered from pain in my knee joints. At sight of the hill, I got enthused. I felt as if I was still in my childhood days. I climbed up the hill as easily as I did in my childhood. Until you have reminded me of pain in my knee joints, it did not even occur to me that I have pain in my knees," said the husband.

57. FARMLAND

A farmer owned a small piece of land. He worked in the field right from the days, when he was very young and his father took him to the field every day along with him. He assisted his father, as long as he was there, and took up the farming independently, after his father was gone. He knew only two places. The places were home where he rested for night and farm where he worked throughout the day. The farmer with his dedication to field work became a part of the farmland.

Many other farmers, who owned lands in neighbourhood of the land owned by the farmer, sold off their lands, relaxed at home and enjoyed no-activity life. They advised the farmer to do what they did. But the farmer did not give in. All thought that the farmer was a sentimental fool.

One day, an interesting discussion took place between the farmer and his wife. The wife said:

"Why don't you sell off the land and rest at home like our neighbours?"

"I shall never do it," said the husband.

"Return from the farm is very less," said the wife.

"I know," said the husband.

"If we sell the land and put sale money in a bank, we shall get better returns out of it," said the wife.

"I know," said the husband.

"Do what is profitable to us," said the wife.

"I shall never do it," said the husband.

"Why?" said the wife.

"I shall be losing employment," said the husband.

"What do you mean?" said the wife.

"My farmland is a source of employment. It is giving me an opportunity to remain employed. If I sell it, I shall lose employment. I do not want to become unemployed, by selling my land," said the husband.

The wife said no more. She got at what her husband hinted at and appreciated him for how he looked at the farmland.

58. AESTHETICS

Management of a big company noticed that there was huge demand for an automobile in market. They decided to develop an automobile that customers desired to have. They set up a design department to design an automobile with many new engineering features. The design team worked hard and produced a design that incorporated many innovative features liked by customers. The management gave green signal for production of the automobile, based on design of their design team.

Very soon, a new automobile with excellent engineering features hit the market. It turned out to be the best in rigidity, safety and fuel economy among its class. But it failed commercially. No customer showed interest to buy the item. In spite of very high level of marketing, sales of the automobile did not pick up in the market. Set back by unexpected turn of events in market, the management stopped production of the automobile and went for an enquiry into why the product failed in market commercially. They called for a meeting of some customers chosen at random and interacted with them. The customers, present in the assembly, one and all, expressed that the automobile released by the Company was an engineering marvel. A Management representative said:

"If you feel that the automobile launched by us is an engineering marvel, what could be the reason why the product is not a success in market?"

"For a product to sell well in market, it is simply not enough for the product to have high end functional features," said a customer.

"What else is required?" said the management representative.

"Look," said the customer.

"Can you explain it more in detail?" said the management representative.

"For a product to sell well, it should be a piece of art combined with engineering marvel. What you produced is an engineering marvel, not a piece of art. Your design team has not followed basic precepts of design," said the customer.

"How do you say so?" said the management representative.

"I am a product developer. Whenever I want to develop a new product, firstly, I visualise how my product must look like. Once I make a model of it and am satisfied with look of my product, I get into building functional features that I want to incorporate in my product, without affecting look of the product. This paves for proper synthesis of art and engineering. In case of your product, your team has bypassed the first step and started off with incorporating various features into the product. Because of this, your product has taken some shape that has resulted out of various features that have gone into the product," said the customer.

The Management realized their mistake and re-launched the product with pleasing look. The product turned out to be a hit away success.

59. CONTROL

At fag end of a financial year, the GM of a Company called for a Production Review Meeting with all concerned departmental heads and reviewed status of production. He was highly disappointed with figures of progress read out by the heads. Every head was short of meeting target fixed for him. The GM expressed his anguish and ire. He said impatiently:

"I am upset with figures given by you. Hardly a month is left before completion of production year and you say there is a long way to go to meet the targets."

"We are in a helpless condition," said one of the heads.

"What is the problem?" said GM.

"There are some people under me, who are creating spokes in production," said the head.

"Why are you not able to control them?" said GM.

"They are powerful. I am not able to control them," said the head.

"Control them or give them to me. I shall control them. I cannot afford to leave them free to spoil the show," said GM.

"I am prepared to give them this instant," said the head.

"We too have some of such candidates in our department," said a second head.

"You too give their names," said GM.

At the instance of the GM, his PA went around and collected slips with names of trouble creators identified by each head. He went to the last head and said:

"Sir, please give me your slip."

"I don't have a list to give you," said the last head.

"But there is one trouble creator in your department, who is known to be a perennial problem for you," said GM.

"Yes, sir," said the last head.

"Give his name," said GM.

"I do not want to give," said the last head.

"Why?" said GM.

"Controlling is my responsibility. It is below my dignity to admit that I have someone with me and I am not able to control him," said the last head.

"That is the spirit. Keep it up," said GM.

Other departmental heads took back the slips given by them and promised to tow the line of the last departmental head.

60. WRONG WINDOW

A king was a great connoisseur of arts. Once in every one year, he held a dazzling function in his state capital and announced awards for virtuosos, who created wonders in their respective fields. The awards carried good titles and prize money that thrilled the awardees. The king constituted committees, which collected names of probable candidates for the awards from each field, shortlisted them and selected the first, second and third in order of merit, in each field. After ratification of the names by the king, announcers announced names of the awardees in the award giving function.

One year, committee on literature collected names of eligible authors for awards, finalised names of three candidate best in order and put up to the king for his approval. The king went through the report prepared by the committee and made some changes in the list of awardees. The committee never faced a situation of that sort in the past. But the committee members did not question jurisprudence of the king.

In the award giving function, names of three best awardees in the field of literature were announced. The announcement caught the audience by surprise. Name of a famous author, who wrote an exceedingly popular book, did not figure in it. The famous author, who was present in the court hall and who expected to be awarded, felt highly dejected and depressed. He did not have cheek to question authority of the king. He was crestfallen. He got up and went out of the function hall.

The famous author did not take the incident lightly. He took it seriously to heart. He felt humiliated to lose his game before a novice, who got award and he did not get it. He decided to end his life and went to a river nearby. He sat on the river bed until evening and proceeded towards the river to walk into it and die. Hardly did the author go a few steps into the river, when someone from behind clutched his shoulder and stopped him. The author looked back and said:

"Who are you?"

"That, I shall tell you later. But tell me why are you trying to end your life?" said the stranger.

"Great injustice is done to me," said the author.

"What injustice is done to you?" said the stranger.

"I am an author. I have not got award and someone, who is a novice before me, got an award. I am not able to digest the defeat," said the author.

"Why did you not get the award?" said the stranger.

"I don't know," said the author.

"Shall I tell you?" said the stranger.

"Please tell me," said the author.

"You wrote a novel by looking at the world through a wrong window," said the stranger.

"What do you mean?" said the author.

"There are before every writer what to write and what not to write. You chose to write what not to write," said the stranger.

"I have written my novel based on what I have seen," said the author.

"I know. You wrote on the life of a sorcerer, who practised rituals of horrific nature in burial grounds and carried out many acts that are bad and spiteful. The way you have run the storyline in the book is very interesting and absorbing. Credit goes to you for that. But know that reading of your book has horrified and sickened many of your readers. Don't you think that you have trespassed into a forbidden zone and selected a storyline for your book that is not good and is detrimental to readers?" said the stranger, in an authoritative tone.

"Who are you?" said the author, taken aback.

"The king," said the stranger.

The author fell flat at feet of the king and requested for his pardon. The king lifted up the author, took him into his embrace and said:

"Look at the world through right window and write what is good and presentable. Never look at the world through wrong window and write what is bad and repulsive."

The author acquiesced in and withdrew from his attempt to end his life. The king and the author walked back homewards. The author followed advice of the king, avoided to look at the world through wrong window, attempted works that were good and became a distinguished litterateur in his life time.

61. POSITION

A factory manufactured a product for a customer. The customer placed a resident inspector in the factory to ensure that the factory produced the product to specifications of the product. The inspector enjoyed high respect in the factory. Every officer in the factory up to head of the institution treated the inspector well and accorded high respect to him. There hardly took place a high level party, without the inspector in it.

The inspector was overwhelmed with respect shown to him. He had the privilege to walk into cabin of the top man without prior appointment, which no other senior executive in the factory enjoyed.

Over the years, the inspector developed a feeling that he enjoyed respect in the factory more than in the organisation for which he worked. One fine morning, he desired to quit the organisation for which he worked and join the factory. He expressed his desire to head of the factory. The head readily accepted to take the inspector. The inspector resigned from services of his organisation and joined the factory. He hoped that respect from factory would continue to be showered on him. But, he found nothing of that sort happening.

On the other hand, the inspector perceived that he lost the privileged position that he enjoyed previously in the factory. It dawned upon him very late to realize that respect rained on him earlier was not due to him, but to the position that he held as representative of the customer.

62. MAGIC MANGO

Every day, a juggler played his tricks of magic in a central square of a busy market place in a town. He chose to do it in afternoons, in lean periods of business hours. He spread a piece of thick linen on ground, put a sack of articles for the show on one side of the linen, kept a little boy nearby, ready to take his commands, made sounds with a sound maker in his hand and called public to witness his show. When the public gathered around the place of show in large numbers, standing in a circle, he started off his show and mesmerised public with his magical tricks. One of the most popular items of his show was planting a mango seed and making it grow into a plant and bear a mango fruit.

A youngster, who worked in a shop in the market place, frequented the place of show, every day. He liked, out of all the items showcased by the juggler, growing of the mango plant that bore fruit, the most. He watched the show keenly in order to know how the juggler did it and how he could do it independently, on his own. But he could not get to know how the juggler played the trick. Many a time, he felt how good it could be, if he knew how to grow mango trees that bore fruits, in no time, as the juggler did. When he could not chase the mystery, he decided to take help from the juggler and said to him, one day, when no one was around:

"I am impressed with your mango fruit trick. Can you teach me how to play it?"

"Why do you want to learn it?" said the juggler.

"I want to grow mangoes, in no time," said the youngster.

"Grow mangos by planting trees that bear fruits," said the juggler.

"That I do not want to do," said the youngster.

"Why?" said the juggler.

"It takes a long time to plant trees and pluck fruits from them. I want to do it the instant way," said the youngster.

"You cannot do it the instant way," said the juggler.

"But you are doing it," said the youngster.

"You too can do it, provided you decide do one thing," said the juggler.

"What is it that I should decide I do?" said the youngster.

"To become a juggler," said the juggler.

The youngster moved away from the place, the very next instant.

63. THE FAIR

A man born and brought up in a small town studied well, became a professional, left the town and went away to a foreign land in search of employment. In the new place of settlement, he rose in his career and became a wealthy man. For a long time, he did not visit his home town. After nearly four decades, he got a call from his childhood friend, to visit his home town on the occasion of a function in his house. The professional was delighted to get the call. He went to his home town. He found joy unbounded to set foot on the soil of his home town, after a very long time.

During the stay in place of his birth, he went to the houses of all his childhood friends, classmates, relatives and acquaintances in the locality, in which he was born and brought up. When he went to the house of a close friend, the friend said:

"Make yourself free today evening."

"What's the matter?" said the professional.

"I shall take you to a fair," said the friend.

"What's the fair?" said the professional.

"There is a fair held in honour of a local god," said the friend.

"Who is the local god?" said the professional.

"He is a great son of the soil," said the friend.

"Don't I know him?" said the professional.

"You know about him," said the friend.

"Who is he?" said the professional.

"He is the man, who used to be the chief guest at annual day function of our school, every year," said the friend.

"The man whom we laughed at and about whom we cut jokes," said the professional, with jeer in his tone.

"Yes," said the friend.

"Why did you choose to make him a god?" said the professional.

"Because he is great," said the friend.

"Are there no other sons of soil, who are great and who could become gods?" said the professional.

"There are many other great men of soil, who are far greater than him. But they are not fit to become gods," said the friend.

"Why do you say so?" said the professional.

"This son of soil, in whose honour the fair is held today, is great because he has rendered great service to society in the town. There are many other sons of soil, who are far greater, but they did nothing to society," said the friend.

The professional had no words in his mouth to speak out.

64. SPOTTING STRENGTHS IN OTHERS

A professional, who was very active in his personal as well as social life, suddenly withdrew himself from all activities and developed philosophical resignation towards life. He stopped moving with his friends and workmates. He kept himself away from his neighbours. He minded his own business and spent rest of the time at home, mostly all alone. His wife was taken aback. She did not understand why such sudden change took over her husband. She tried to elicit truth from her husband. But the professional revealed nothing. He brushed aside when his wife doubted if there was any problem with anyone of his friends.

Slowly, the effect of withdrawal from all activities started telling upon health of the professional. Most of the times, when he was alone, he got into thoughtful rumination and brooded over something. His wife was worried. She decided to get into action. She sat with her husband, one day, and said to him:

"Of late, you are not moving out with anyone. What is the matter?"

"There is nothing specific," said the husband, taking lightly question of his wife.

"There is something. You must tell me," persisted the wife.

"What shall I tell you? I feel sorry to realize lately that I have no friend, who does not have a quality that I don't like. Everyone has some or other defect that I don't like," said the husband.

"There is nothing unusual about it. It is but natural that everyone born on this earth has some or other defect. There can be none who is absolutely flawless," said the wife.

"When I find fault in someone, I feel like detesting him and moving away from him," said the husband.

"Don't see the fault to stop detesting and moving away from him," said the wife.

"What else can I do?" said the husband.

"See what you like that keeps you connected to your friend," said the wife.

The professional realized his mistake, thanked his wife and started looking out for qualities that he liked in his friends rather than looking out for qualities that he abhorred. Very soon, he was back to his usual self, with a pleasant demeanour.

65. TRAFFIC POLICE

The population of a city grew enormously. Bulging with it, the city expanded far and wide. Many cross road junctions and traffic points came up every here and there, all over the city. Scenes of traffic with pedestrians, bicycles, tricycles, cars, buses and other modes of transport, vying for space and being jam-packed, became very common and order of the day. No traffic point went well, without a traffic constable there constantly standing guard, regulating flow of traffic and manning the junction. Even if the constable missed in his place for a brief while, the traffic went awry and got stuck. The rushing public respected traffic rules, if they saw the constable in his place. Otherwise, they threw rules to winds and went as they liked.

The city police administration found it very difficult to meet demand of traffic police, with ever increasing traffic and severe crunch of constabulary. Periodic recruitment of additional constabulary too did not resolve the problem fully. The head of the police convened a meeting with his subordinate officers, to elicit their opinions on how to tide over the situation. He said:

"We are not able to meet demand of deploying more and more traffic constables at traffic points. What shall we do?"

"Can we not recruit additional manpower?" said one cop.

"That we are doing from time to time. In spite of it, we are not able to meet the load. Rate of increase of traffic is outmatching rate of recruitment of staff," said head of the police.

"I have a suggestion," said a young cop.

"What is it?" said head of the police.

"Let us install CC cameras at all cross road junctions and put up boards that 'You are under surveillance of CC cameras'," said the young cop.

"How does it help?" said head of the police.

"For fear of being caught on CC cameras, no one will dare violate traffic rules," said the young cop.

"I don't think that we have enough number of CC cameras for installation at all road joints," said head of the police.

"It doesn't matter. Displaying boards 'You are under surveillance of CC cameras' suffices," said the young cop.

The head smiled at path finding suggestion given by the young cop and extolled him. Implementation of the suggestion helped solve the traffic problem to a large extent.

66. RENUNCIATION

People in a forest tribe built a temple in the name of a great man from their clan, who renounced the world, went away to the Himalayas and attained heavenly bliss. The forest dwellers, in remembrance of the great man, held a large fair, every year, and celebrated the event with great gusto.

A family man from the tribe got inspired by the great man, for whom the temple was erected. He surmised that the man became great, because he renounced the world. He too decided to renounce the world and become great.

One day, he renounced the world and went away into oblivion. After many years, he returned to his place of birth to see, if people of his land constructed a temple in his name. When nothing of sort happened, he was surprised and aggrieved. He went to the headman to express his resentment. He said to the headman:

"People of this land are partial."

"What makes you say so?" said the headman.

"You have constructed a temple in the name of a man from our tribe, who renounced the world. You have not done the same to me, even though I too renounced the world," said the man.

"But there is a subtle difference between why the saint renounced the world and why you renounced the world," said the headman.

"What is it?" said the man.

"The saint renounced the world for a holy cause in life. You renounced the world to escape your worldly responsibilities," said the headman.

The man, with downcast eyes, left from presence of the headman.

67. TOGETHERNESS

A householder had two milk yielding buffaloes in his house. One of the buffaloes was docile, calm going and old. The second one was young and highly agile. On one rainy day, the young buffalo slipped on smooth flooring of the house in which she lived and suffered a serious injury in one of her rear legs. Over a period of time, the injury got healed, but the poor buffalo limped.

Son of the householder was a school going boy. During his leisure times, he took both the buffaloes for grazing to nearby open lands. He grazed the cattle until evening and brought them back by dusk fall.

One day, when the two buffaloes grazed in a grazing ground, another buffalo that grazed nearby got suddenly volatile, ran charging towards the old buffalo and attacked her. The poor old buffalo, half unprepared for sudden attack by the rogue buffalo and half unable to fight back, suffered helplessly from repeated attacks of the attacker. The young buffalo, which grazed close by, did not take the attack lightly. She ran limping to rescue of the old one, charged at the attacker ferociously and chased her away. The boy, who strolled nearby, watched the scene with abated breath and wondered at the spirit of camaraderie shown by the young buffalo. He went to the young one, patted on her back and consoled the old one that came under attack. He felt like staying no more there and drove the cattle back home much before, that day. When he narrated the episode, everyone in the house wondered for the concern shown by the heroic young buffalo.

After a few months, the householder decided to sell off the old buffalo in cattle fair. When the boy came to know of it, he turned sad. He pleaded with his parents not to separate the comrades. But the elders laughed away sentimental attachment of the boy. The householder conducted the old buffalo to cattle fair, the next day morning, and sold her off in the fair. The boy looked on pensively, when the old buffalo walked away from his house.

Later, the boy, highly melancholy, took the young one to grazing ground. But the young one did not touch the grass. She was highly touched. The boy wept outwardly and the young buffalo did it inwardly.

68. SUN RISE

A farmer faced a problem with his son. He was worried. He went to a physician in his village and poured out his woes to him. The physician said:

"Tell me plainly what problem are you facing with your son?"

"He gets up very late in the morning," said the farmer.

"Why do you think that it is a serious problem," said the physician.

"What more serious problem than this can be there for a farmer? Because of this problem, my son is not able to attend to farming job in fields effectively," said the farmer.

"Did you not advise your son?" said the physician.

"I did. But my son is not heeding me," said the farmer.

"What do you want from me?" said the physician.

"I want a medicine for my son to get out of getting up late in mornings," said the farmer.

"Send your son to me. I shall give him a medicine," said the physician.

The farmer sent his son to the physician on some pretext. The physician said to son of the farmer:

"Young man, can you do me a favour?"

"What shall I do for you, sir," said son of the farmer.

"I have prepared a wonder-medicine from medicinal plants for enhanced health and vigour in life. According to books on medicine, the medicine will work, only if it is exposed to sunrays just before sunrise. From within our village, we are able to see the sun only after sunrise. Is it possible for you to take me into open fields, from where I can expose my medicine to sunrays before sunrise?" said the physician.

"I can do it," conceded son of the farmer.

"Well, thank you. Shall we start our job from tomorrow onwards?" said the physician.

"Sure," said son of the farmer.

For the next few weeks, the physician and son of the farmer went to the fields regularly, much before daybreak. The physician did his job. He exposed his medicine to rays coming from the sun, before the sun arose. Son of the farmer had no work. He stayed nearby, watching celestial beauty of the sun rising above horizon and illuminating the world. After his job was over, the physician gave a portion of the potion to son of the farmer and asked him to drink it. Son of the farmer took it. When the physician stopped going to the fields, wife of the physician said to the physician:

"You stopped going to fields. Is your job over?"

"Yes," said the physician.

"The farmer wanted a medicine to be given to his son. Did you prepare it?" said wife of the physician.

"I prepared and made son of the farmer drink it, as well," said the physician.

"Why did you expose the medicine to sunrise?" said wife of the physician.

"I have not exposed any medicine to sunrise," said the physician.

"What else did you do?" said wife of the physician.

"I exposed son of the farmer to sunrise," said the physician.

Wife of the physician failed to understand her mystic husband. She cast on him glances that indicated that she did not understand him and went away inside the house. Meantime, the farmer called on the physician and said:

"Thank you."

"Is my medicine working?" said the physician.

"It is working wonderfully well. After taking the medicine, my son is getting up much before daybreak and going to fields," said the farmer.

"That is very satisfying to learn about," said the physician.

The farmer thanked the physician once again and went away. The physician acknowledged thanks of the farmer and leaned back in his easy chair to muse. He did not reveal to anyone that the real medicine what he gave to son of the farmer was giving him a taste of beauty before day break and create longing in him to enjoy it again and again.

69. WORK HOME

A philanthropist opened an old age home in a city. Inmates of the home were pretty old. But they were markedly happy. A medical practitioner, who visited a few old age homes in the city, regularly paid a visit to the old age home run by the philanthropist. One day, the doctor said to the philanthropist:

"I want to tell something about your home."

"Tell me doctor," said the philanthropist.

"I am visiting quite a few old age homes in the city. Wherever I go, I find inmates of the homes coming to me with various ailments. I see inmates there very desolate, deserted, depressed and inactive. But in case of your home, I hardly find people coming to me with ailments. They are always happy, healthy, lively and brimming with activity. I rarely have the need to treat them," said the doctor.

"I know," said the philanthropist.

"I want to know what you are doing to keep inmates of your home healthy and happy," said the doctor.

"I make them work," said the philanthropist.

70. CREATOR'S WORKSHOP

A sculptor worked on creation of a beautiful shrine in a valley formed out of three hills. He built the shrine in a picturesque locale that teemed with natural beauty.

He resided in a cave dwelling nearby and worked on his project with great dedication. He worked day and night. The shrine took the shape of a thing of beauty under master strokes of the carver.

One day, god happened to go by the place, where the creator created the shrine. He was highly pleased with works of beauty created by the creator. He appeared before the creator and said:

"I am highly pleased with your creations. Come with me. I shall take you to the paradise."

"What is paradise?" said the creator.

"A place, where you need not work and there is pleasure available everywhere there," said the god.

"I do not want to come there," said the creator.

"Why?" said the god.

"The place where I have no work to do is not a paradise for me," said the creator.

The god disappeared. The creator, after many years, died. He went to stand in the court of Yama, the celestial celebrity, who pronounced judgements for mortals after their death, based on good and bad deeds done by them. Yama said to the creator:

"You have done good deeds. Go to paradise."

"I don't want to go there," said the creator.

"I understand you denied going to paradise earlier too," said Yama.

"Yes," said the creator.

"If you do not want to go to paradise, tell me where do you want to go? I can't keep you here, because this is a hell meant for people, who have done bad deeds," said Yama.

"Send me back to earth," said the creator.

"Why?" said Yama.

"There is work for me to do there," said the creator.

Yama, the great dispenser of justice, smiled and sent the creator back to the place, where he wanted to work.

71. RITUALS

A man born in an orthodox family never followed any rituals that his family followed customarily. He did not believe in rituals. He propagated against them. His father died. His mother asked him to observe after-death-rituals for his father. The man did not object. He performed all rituals, which were followed traditionally in his family, methodically, regularly and religiously. His mother was pleased. One day, a friend of the man remarked:

"You are changed."

"What way am I changed?" said the man.

"You never believed in rituals. But you are following them now," said the friend.

"You are right," said the man.

"Have you started believing in the rituals?" said the friend.

"I have no belief in rituals," said the man.

"If that is the case, why are you following them?" said the friend.

"I love my mother. I do not want her to develop a feeling that I am not following rituals and therefore not paying due respect to my father after his death. I have followed the rituals to create a feeling of satisfaction in my mother that I follow tradition and shall continue to do so in future to remember and respect departed souls in my family," said the man.

72. WISE WIFE

A husband and his wife went with a group of travellers, on a sightseeing trip. The husband was a miser. He avoided purchases as far as possible. The wife was the other way round. She was a spendthrift. Wherever she went, she made purchases liberally, immaterial whether the items purchased were of use or not. She knew that her husband disapproved of her way of wasting money. As far as possible, she took care to make the purchases, during the times, when her husband was not nearby. She paid for the purchases from the money that carried secretly with her.

One day, the travellers went on tour to a big city. They toured the city from morning to evening, and, at end of their tour, they went to a market that was very big. In the market place, men and women separated out. The men moved about in lanes and by lanes of the market, watching curiously articles displayed in shops on either side of the walkways. The womenfolk excused themselves into the area where materials for women were sold. With her husband away, the wife got free to buy whatever she wanted. She purchased a lot that virtually cost a fortune.

Hardly did she finish her purchasing and put her hand into her hand bag to take out money, when suddenly her husband thrust upon the scene from behind. The wife got panicky. She understood that she was caught red-handedly. She did not like to lose out. She said immediately to her husband, with full presence of mind:

"I am very happy, you have come."

"Why? What happened?" said the husband.

"I made some purchases. Please make the payment," said the wife.

The husband was in a fix. He could not decide whether to pay for the purchases or not. He looked around. He saw many ladies of his travel party standing around his wife. He found it very awkward to refuse to pay in presence of the ladies. For the sake of prestige, which he cursed, he took out his purse, paid the bill silently, collected the package of purchases and went behind his wife. He felt that he should not have come to that spot.

73. OUR PEOPLE

The king of a small nation went on the mission of a conquest. He invaded many neighbouring nations, fought wars, defeated kings of the nations and brought many lands under his control. He became an emperor and ruled from a capital that was in the centre of his monarchy. He constituted a cabinet of courtiers and ruled under their able guidance.

C. N. Nageswara Rao

The king had a judge in his court. The judge was a man of great wisdom. He was in good books of the emperor, since he worked earlier in court of the emperor, when the emperor was a small king, and won his admiration for his land mark judgements. The emperor treated the judge with high respect.

Now and then, the king received complaints that the judge was partial and he favoured some people. Initially the king did not give much of credence to the complaints, because he knew about the judge earlier. But when the complaints came again and again, the emperor decided to look into the matter and find out reality in the complaints. He called the judge into his private chamber and said to him:

"I am given to understand that you are partial to some people and not dispensing justice equally to all."

"I admit it," said the judge.

"What is the reason for it?" said the king.

"I am partial to people who are from our kingdom," said the judge.

"What do you mean by our kingdom?" said the king.

"The kingdom that you ruled earlier before becoming emperor of this vast empire," said the judge.

The king understood why the judge was partial. He said:

"Now I understand why you are partial to people of our kingdom," said the king.

"Thank you," said the judge.

"But there is a point for you to note," said the king.

"What is it?" said the judge.

"Our people are not the people that are from our erstwhile kingdom," said the king.

"Then?" said the judge.

"Our people are all the people that are from our entire empire. I am no more king of a small kingdom, but emperor of a big empire," said the king.

The judge stood corrected. He changed his mind set and dispensed justice equally to all.

74. HUMAN PSYCHOLOGY

Labourers that sought to be employed on daily wages assembled in a centre in a busy market place. People in need of the labourers visited the centre, saw for labourers who could do their jobs, negotiated, for wages to be paid, with the labourers that volunteered to do their jobs, struck deals and took the labourers to be employed, along with them.

Two middle aged labourers living in a slum came regularly to the centre. Out of them, one person was invariably employed, every day, by one or other employer. The second person found it very difficult to get employed. Many a time, he returned home with none employing him for the day. He wondered how the first man with him got employed immediately and he was not employed. One day, he said to the first person:

"I want to know one secret from you."

"What is it?" said the first person.

"You get employed every day without fail and I return home without employment, many times. What is the reason?" said the second person.

"I shall tell you, if you don't feel bad," said the first person.

"Please tell me," said the second person.

"Many people, who come to employ me, invariably offer less than what I ask for. I don't demand what I ask for. I agree for what they offer and go with them to do their job. Whereas, you stick to what you ask for and refuge to do the job, unless what you have asked for is given by the employer," said the first person.

"If you agree to work for less offers, don't you lose out?" said the second person.

"No," said the first person.

"How?" said the second person.

"After completion of job given to me, I ask my employer to give me more and invariably he gives me more than what I have asked for initially," said the first person.

"Why does the employer offer less than what you have asked for initially and give you more in the end," said the second person.

"That is human psychology," said the first person.

The second person learnt from his friend to get employed every day, without fail.

75. DREAMS

Two young men set out separately from their homes in search of employment. On way to their destinations, they happened to stay together for a couple of days, in a wayside inn. They introduced themselves to each other, knew about what for they set out from their homes and where they headed towards. During their stay in the inn, they moved around everywhere together, and became good friends.

The night before they were to check out of the inn, both the young men had very interesting dreams. When they got up after day break, they recollected the dreams that they had and revealed them to each other. First one said:

"I had a wonderful dream yester night. I visited a temple complex, in which there were many shrines dedicated to various deities. Hardly did I go into the temple complex, when evening lamps in the shrines came on, one after another, and under bright light of the lamps, idols of the presiding deities, bedecked with stone studded gold ornaments, glowed resplendently. It appeared to me as if the deities blessed me and I was in for good success in my life."

"It is really by sheer coincidence. I too had a similar dream. Today, just before day break, when I was fast asleep, a goddess appeared in my dream, offered to me a bowl full of porridge and asked me to have it. I had the porridge. I felt that the goddess showered on me her benediction," said the second one.

Both young men congratulated each other for nice and uplifting dreams that they had, told each other that their dreams would become reality very soon, checked out of the inn and went on their way to their respective destinations.

After ten years, the friends met with each other, accidentally in a village fair. They recognised each other and, after exchange of greetings, fell into conversation. The first one said:

"How are you?"

"I am fine. I am doing well. I tried for a job. I could not get it. I started a small business in a village nearby. The business has clicked. I am earning more than I have expected. The dream that I had in the inn has realized. How about you?" said the second one.

"My dream has not come true," said the first one, sadly.

"My dream too did not come true by itself. I struggled hard to make it come true," said the second one.

"I did nothing of that sort," said the first one.

"Do what I have done. Your dream too will come true," said the second one.

The first one understood that the dream that he had would not materialize by itself, he would have to make it materialize and got into action to make it materialize.

76. THE THIEF

A young man left home in his village and migrated to a city nearby, in search of gainful employment. He heard that there were many jobs in the city and he could lay his hands on one of them no sooner than he arrived in the city. But what he heard did not turn out to be true. However hard the man tried to do a job that he could do, he did not get. He was highly disappointed. He did not like to go back home and say that he could not get employment in the city. He was in a dilemma. He did not know what to do. He chose to stay in a hut in a slum, for a paltry rent, and managed to support himself with little money that he had with him. He lived in utter misery.

Over the days, the young man went into wrong hands. He became close to a circle of thieves. The thieves took the man into their gang, trained him in how to commit petty thefts and made him a skilled thief. The man, converted into being a thief, earned his livelihood by thieving and lived in the company of thieves.

One day, leader of the gang took the man to a residential locality, showed him a house there and said to him:

"Owner of this house is away from home. His wife is all alone in the house. It is the best time for us to commit the theft in this house. Take one more accomplice from our gang with you and commit theft in this house tonight."

"I shall not do it," said the young man, resolutely.

"Why will you not do it?" said the gang leader, taken aback.

"When I went without food, I had it from lady of this house. I cannot steal in a house that fed me," said the young man.

"Thieves should not be sentimental," said the gang leader.

"But, I am sentimental," said the young man.

The young man did not wait for any more response from the gang leader. He turned away from him, went home, collected his belongings, vacated the hut and went back to his village to lead a dignified life that he led earlier. Before leaving the city, he met lady of the house, where he was asked to commit theft, and alerted her about a possible theft by some unknown thieves, in her house.

77. DOING NOTHING

A boss in a factory had a subordinate. The subordinate was very good at work. He did every type of job assigned to him meticulously well and very fast. He never idled. He was very busy, doing something or other, all throughout his stay in office. The boss immensely liked his subordinate. Both went together very well.

The boss observed one thing very odd in his subordinate. However busy the subordinate was and however hard he worked during office hours, he was never tired. He remained as active at end of shift as at start of it, all throughout weekdays. But he appeared highly tired and inactive, whenever he reported to office, after a holiday or weekend. The boss could not guess what could be the problem. One day, out of curiosity, he broached the subject with the subordinate:

"If you don't feel bad, I shall ask you one question."

"Please ask me, sir," said the subordinate.

"Whenever you come to office after a holiday, I see you highly exhausted. What is the reason? By chance, do you work more on holidays?" said the boss.

"You touched upon a very important subject, sir. In fact, I myself fail to understand why I get highly tired after a holiday. The fact is I just don't do anything on a holiday, other than resting and whiling away time, doing nothing," said the subordinate.

"Don't you do anything on a holiday?" said the boss.

"Absolutely nothing," said the subordinate.

"And you get exhausted by doing nothing," said the boss.

"Yes, sir," said the subordinate.

"Now I know the reason why you get exhausted," said the boss.

"What is it, sir?" said the subordinate.

"Resting, doing nothing," said the boss.

"How can I get exhausted by doing nothing?" said the subordinate.

"Resting by doing nothing is more exhaustive than doing something," said the boss.

The subordinate learnt to remain busy on holidays too and drove away exhaustion from his life.

78. TURN OF EVENTS

A householder was stricken with grief. He faced many problems, all at a time. His job was at stake. His wife was not keeping well. His son did not come up in life. His married daughter faced problems from her in-laws. He found it very difficult to overcome the problems that surrounded him, all of a sudden. He thought about how to come out of the troubles. But he found no way out. He became weary. He was vexed with life. He arrived at a conclusion that ending life was far more desirable than leading a life with many insolvable problems.

One day, at noon, he went to a river nearby, with a serious resolve to jump down into it and die. He saw some people taking bath in the river and moving about by the riverside. He decided to wait until the people in the place went away and he was all alone there. He sat on a step in a flight of steps that led down to water in the river. He saw the river into which he was to get into. The river, unmindful of what was there in his mind, went down its course calmly, making absolutely no noise. People in the place left one by one. An angler, who cast his fishing net in the river to catch fish, hauled back the net, collected the fish caught in it, transferred them into a wicker basket with a lid on it and went away, in the last, with his fishing paraphernalia. The householder looked around and ensured for himself that he was all alone and there was no other person in the place. He got up with a firm resolve to walk down into the river and die.

He climbed down, step after step, and went ankle deep into the river. He stood there unmoved for a minute, to take a call and bid adieu to his life. He thought for the last, decided his course of action and moved forward deeper into the running waters. Just before he drowned himself into the river, he noticed that a woman came running from behind and jumped into the river, just by the side of him, and water in the river splashed around heavily with a big sound. The householder, though on his way to death, got panicky with the sudden development and watched with horror what happened. He found that the woman was caught in running current of the river and getting washed away. He did not let it happen. He leaped forward, caught the lady by her hair, dragged her back and saved her. She brought the lady to the shore, attended on her until she returned to her consciousness, admonished her for her foolish act and put good sense in her to go back home. He escorted the lady to her house and handed her over to her family members.

After the incident, the householder walked back homewards merrily. He was very happy to feel that he was lucky enough to be present at the site, when the lady attempted her suicide and he saved her from being washed away. He walked under hot sun. He hastened his steps to reach home fast. He forgot to die.

79. PROMISE

A farmer fell seriously sick. He understood that he would not live long. He called his wife and son to his bedside and said:

"I have a request to make to you."

"What is it?" said the boy.

"The land what we are tilling today is with us for the last three hundred years. I am given to understand that the land was gifted to one of our forefathers for a valorous act that he did. Do never sell it. Let it always remain with our family," said the farmer.

"I shall do it," said son of the farmer.

But the boy broke his promise. He sold off the land and spent returns out of the sales on medical treatment of his father. But the farmer did not survive. The boy became fatherless and landless. He did not repent. He had satisfaction that he did not spare any efforts to save his father, even at the cost of the land.

The boy grew up into a young man. He worked hard to come up in life. He earned money. He became rich, over a period of time. He went back to the buyer, who bought the land from him, and requested him to sell the land back to him. The buyer knew sentiment of the farmer's son and quoted very high for the land. Son of the farmer did not hesitate. He shelved good part of his wealth and took the land back into his possession. His mother was very unhappy. She commented:

"You took a wrong decision."

"Why?" said son of the farmer.

"You paid a fortune for the land that you bought. For the money you spent, you could have got much bigger land elsewhere," said the mother.

"Had I bought land elsewhere, I could not have kept up the word that I gave to my father. With the purchase of our own land back, I am happy, I kept up promise given to my father," said son of the farmer.

The mother was very happy with action of her son.

80. CELEBRATION

A man after retirement was in a mood of high celebration. He hosted a big party to his friends and relatives. One of the friends said:

"You are feeling highly jubilant."

"That I am," said the retiree.

"Normally people after retirement feel very sad. But you are other way round," said the friend.

"Yes," said the retiree.

"What is the reason?" said the friend.

"During my service, I never worked. I am celebrating that," said the retiree.

"What do you mean?" said the friend.

"What I say is true. During my entire service spanning over more than four decades, I managed my job, without doing any work," said the retiree.

"How could you manage doing nothing?" said the friend.

"Instead of managing my work, I managed my bosses," said the retiree.

"Can you please elaborate?" said the friend.

"I heaped praises on hard working officers and gave them the impression that I liked the hard working. I gave tons of advices to people and gave them the impression that I was very knowledgeable. I carried news to officers about what others thought about them and won their hearts. I catered to personal needs of people, who solicited my help. I spoke the language that people liked. I left impression in many people that I was a moving force that did great service to the organisation. None of my bosses ever asked me to do any job, since I was very close to the top echelon," said the retiree.

The party was over. Everybody in the party praised the retiree for his cleverness. Everyone dispersed for the day. Next day, the retiree appeared very sad. One of his friends, who saw him very happy the previous day, wondered for such sudden change and asked him:

"What is the matter? You were very happy yesterday and you are very sad today."

"I had a dream yesterday, which has made me unhappy," said the retiree.

"What did you see in the dream?" said the friend.

"I saw in my dream the organisation, in which I worked, jumping in joy, in celebration of my retirement," said the retiree.

81. IDOL WORSHIP

People of an ancient kingdom were highly devout. They strongly believed that god existed and prayed to god in iconic form of idols in places of worship. They carried out many rituals regularly and religiously with the fond hope that the god would be pleased with their worship and he would help realize their wishes.

There lived in the same kingdom some other people, who strongly condemned idol worship. They held the view that worshipping idols was nothing short of a blind belief.

A philosopher in the kingdom propagated that the god was omnipresent and strongly condemned idol worship. People that supported idol worship denounced the philosopher and people that were against idol worship supported the philosopher and became his staunch followers. Over a period of time, followers for the philosopher increased many-fold and countered the idol worshippers.

At end of his life, the philosopher left for heavenly bliss. Followers of the philosopher turned very sad. They could not get adjusted to the void that the great philosopher left in their lives. They thought of many ways how they could commemorate the great departed soul. They erected a great place of worship, installed idol of the philosopher in it and worshipped the philosopher in iconic form of the idol.

82. RUMOUR

The fort of a king came under sudden attack by an invader. A fierce battle ensued. Forces of the king fought a pitched war from within the fort and those of the invader fought from outside of it. Forces of the king were limited in numbers. They were ill equipped with arms, ammunition and other resources. Still they boldly faced a war that was virtually thrust upon them. They staked their lives and fought ferociously to save their peace loving king and their motherland. Forces of the invader, more in number, well equipped and well prepared, fought from outside the fort to lay seize to the fort at any cost.

The war continued in intermittent spells for many days. Chief Minister of the king noticed that, day by day, the enemy forces gained upper hand and spirits of his own forces were on wane. He understood that the fight could not continue for long and fall of the fort appeared imminent. He was a wise man. He did not lose courage. He did not like to lose out to his enemy easily. He conceived of a two pronged strategy to boost falling spirits of his forces and to check rising spirits of the enemy forces. He put his idea into action. He called a trust worthy soldier and said to him:

"Escape out of the fort by a secret passage. Once you surface out of the passage, manage a horse from some source, mount it and come back to the fort, as if stealthily. Ensure that the enemy forces spot you and you get caught. In case they catch you and force you to reveal about you, tell them that you went on a royal mission to neighbouring kings seeking their help and the neighbouring kings have condescended to send large contingents of their armed forces in a couple of days."

The courier did as per instructions of the chief minister. He allowed himself to be caught by enemy forces. In the interrogation, he revealed that he went with a message to neighbouring kings, the kings agreed to send their forces and the forces of the neighbouring kings were on their way to the fort. A wave of panic started in the enemy camp. The invader, who was highly confident of his victory, was taken aback by the sudden turn of events. He was in split mind as to what to do.

Meantime, the chief minister engineered spreading out a rumour among his own forces that neighbouring kings sent their troupes to help them. The rumour had a telling effect on the defending forces. The armed forces, with the hope that additional forces would join them soon, fought war with renewed energy and fortified spirit. They shattered confidence of the enemy forces and made them flee away. The strategy of the chief minister worked wonders.

83. TWO HEROES

The king of a kingdom died, all of a sudden. He left no heir apparent to the throne. The dynasty that ruled the kingdom for many generations ended. The royal establishment that was in its place for centuries broke down. With no ruler sitting on the throne, anarchy set in the kingdom. Lawlessness took its toll. People became free to do whatever they liked. Persons of various beliefs and ideologies segregated into discrete groups and warred with one another. Society that remained cohesive for a long time disintegrated. The kingdom slid into big turmoil. Some distant relatives of the erstwhile king occupied the throne, one after another, and made abortive bid to establish their rule. But, they, in quick succession, died in internal coups, hatched by power mongers. Disunity took roots in the kingdom. Kings of neighbouring realms prepared to invade the kingdom. The kingdom stood at a great risk of extinction.

A patriot in army of the kingdom, who watched happenings in the kingdom for a long time, perceived that the kingdom could lose its sovereignty any time and slip into hands of enemies. He decided not to allow that to happen. He got into action. He designed a strategy and, with the support of some people in the kingdom, managed to capture power in the kingdom. He sat on the throne, in an air of uncertainty, and started his rule.

Aspirants, who had an eye on the throne and who tried and failed to get it, tried in many ways to destabilize rule of the patriot. They incited public, spearheaded movements against the king and created unrest in society. The new king tried his best to bring law and order situation under his control, by all possible democratic means. But when his efforts failed to yield desired results, he changed gear and switched over to autocracy. For the purpose of stability in his rule, he used all means to crush rebels and dissenters that waged war against the crown. In the process, many people, who were against the king, kissed dust and perished. It took many years and cost many lives for the king to usher in stability in the kingdom. During the period, the king escaped many coups on his life and survived by sheer stroke of luck. He turned out to be a great dictator.

One day, a great saint from the kingdom sought interview with the king. The king granted the interview. The saint met the king and said:

"You have mercilessly killed many people in the kingdom. Your conscience will smite you for your misdeeds."

"My conscience will never smite me," said the king.

"Why?" said the saint.

"I have done it for a purpose. Had I not done it, this great kingdom would have gone into oblivion. I prevented that from happening. I am not repenting for what I have done," said the king.

The saint was satisfied. He blessed the king and went away. He felt that he saw a great king in his life.

84. BOSS

A senior officer was head of a production department. He had a big office with table, side rack, cupboard, telephones, buzzers, clerk cum typist and a messenger. The senior officer was very busy from morning to evening with attending telephone calls, receiving visitors, interacting with union leaders, conducting review meetings and going on visits to shop floors, every now and then. He discharged his duties scrupulously well. He commanded respect from subordinates, colleagues and superiors, all alike.

A junior officer, next in command to the head, down the line, was a man of different stuff. He did not do his job properly. He tried to do the job of his boss. He envied the status enjoyed by his boss. He always dreamt of becoming a boss, occupying the seat held by his boss and enjoying comforts enjoyed by him. Whenever he got an opportunity to act as in-charge in place of his boss, he overacted as a boss. He learnt to act more as a boss than as a subordinate.

Unfortunately, the junior officer never got the opportunity to become permanent head of the department. He continued to report to his senior officer, until the senior officer became General Manager of the organisation and a new senior officer took the place vacated by him as a departmental head. The junior officer, second in command earlier, continued to remain second in command, even after change of head. His dream to become departmental head did not materialize. He remained crestfallen.

One day, the General Manager met a batch of young engineers that newly joined the organisation, in auditorium, for an interactive session, and addressed them:

"My dear young engineers, I know very well that you have joined this organisation with many hopes and aspirations. In the days to come, you will become senior officers and become bosses of your respective areas. In this regard, I wish to give you one piece of advice. That is if you want to become good bosses, learn how to be good subordinates. If you don't to know how to act like good subordinates, remember that you will never become good bosses."

When a young recruit requested the General Manager to elaborate on the issue, the General Manager said:

"If you learn to be a good subordinate, your boss will like you and make you boss, one day. Once you become a boss, your subordinates will be subordinate to you, because you were subordinate to your boss earlier. On the other hand, if you do not learn to be a good subordinate, your boss will not like you and will never make you boss. Even if you become a boss, your subordinates will not be subordinate to you, because you were not subordinate to your boss earlier."

The junior officer, who remained second in command for a long time under the General Manager, earlier, understood that the General Manager delivered his address keeping him in his mind, got up silently from his seat and went out of the auditorium.

85. THE VEDAS

A teacher ran a school in serene environs of a forest. He taught the Vedas to his disciples. Every day, he took his students to a hillside stream for morning ablutions and, after ablutions, made the students render sonorously the Vedas in a group. The symphony of sounds created by confluence of many young voices feasted ears of hearers. The melodious intonation, in agreement with sounds of music enshrined in lyrically composed verses of the Vedas, released waves of magic that spread out splendour in serene environs of the streamside.

Every day, when the rendition was on, a tribal boy came from somewhere, sat underneath a massive tree nearby and listened to chanting of the Vedas ecstatically. The teacher noticed the boy. But he paid no attention to him for a long time. However, when the boy made his presence regularly to listen to the musical rendition, for many days on end, the teacher grew curious about the boy, went to him sitting under the tree and said to him:

"I see you sitting under the tree, every day. What are you doing here?"

"I come here to listen to the musical rendition," said the tribal boy.

"Do you know anything about the Vedas?" said the teacher.

"What are Vedas?" said the tribal boy.

"What you are listening to?" said the teacher.

"I don't know," said the tribal boy.

"If that is the case, what for you listening to the Vedas?" said the teacher.

"I don't know what I am listening to. I only know that I am listening to sounds of music that are pleasant to my ears," said the tribal boy.

The teacher understood what for the tribal boy listened to the rendition. He let the tribal boy blissfully enjoy what he liked. He bowed his head low in reverence to the creators that composed things of beauty in the form of the Vedas.

86. HUMAN RACE

An educated man turned very sad to notice various evils that plagued human society. He wondered how greed, rivalry, desire for supremacy, discontentment, exploitation, hating and many other vile qualities adversely affected human society and turned one person against another. He felt very bad about human society, which virtually disintegrated into individuals physically living together in one place, but wholly disconnected from one another. He thought that animal world, with better social bonding, was far superior to human society. He concluded for himself that he could not pull on living the life of a human being anymore and he should opt to lead the life of any living creature on earth other than that of a human being. He walked to the god and said to him:

"Turn me into being any living creature on earth other than human being."

"Your desire is very strange," said the god.

"Why do you say so?" said the man.

"Of all living species on earth, human race is the best," said the god.

"I don't agree," said the man.

"Why?" said the god.

"Human society has lost its illustrious standing. It has fallen from a glorious top to abysmal bottom. It has turned from being good to bad. It is riddled with many undesirable qualities," said the man.

"But you have missed to note that it is still crowned with one great quality," said the god.

"What is it?" said the man.

"Heroes are worshipped, villains are cursed and triumph of good over bad is celebrated. This is the case everywhere, in all walks of life, all over the globe. What more credentials do you want to testify that human society is very great," said the god.

The educated man saw what he missed to see hitherto, took leave of the preceptor in the form of god and went back to live like an ideal individual in human society.

87. THE FIGHTER

In good olden days, a cruel king ruled a kingdom. He was very unkind. He patronised a sport in which two fighters fought a duel with swords in their hands and the fight continued until one fighter killed another fighter in the fight. The fight took place in a huge court, surrounded by a gallery, running all around. Spectators, mostly nobles, courtiers in service of the king and kith and kin of the royalty watched the fight gleefully, with abated breath from seats in galleries. They rejoiced uproariously, when one fighter established one-upmanship over his rival and the loser fell, bled and died. It was a sport to revel in for the royal blood and life and death issue for the fighters that fought the duel.

The event took place regularly and every time, it took place at the cost of life of a fighter. With scant respect for human life, the organisers organised the event, just because the king liked the event. The fighters staked their lives and fought, because the fight carried hefty prize money and whosoever won in the fight got rewarded richly by the king. However, many fighters felt strongly in their hearts that continuing the fight until one fighter killed the other was unkind and the duel should stop short of killing. But knowing cruel mind of the king, no one dared speak out. The ugly sport continued costing life of one fighter, every time it was fought.

Once, there was an occasion for celebration in the royal household. Many dignitaries from outside of the kingdom made their presence in the celebrations. The king wanted a duel to be organised. The organisers organised the event. Two ferocious fighters, with shining swords in their hands, rushed into well of the court, with serious determination to kill each other. The spectators, sitting in their places in the galleries, watched the scene down below, to unleash very soon. The bloody fight started.

After a long drawn fight that entertained the onlookers, one of the fighters, bruised badly, fell down on ground and the winner stood triumphantly with his blood stained sword marked at chest of the loser. The onlookers looked curiously and expectantly for the winner to finish off the loser. But the winner stood steadily unmoved from his position. He neither did pierce the sword into chest of his rival, nor did he lift it off. Nerve breaking tension gripped the onlookers. The spectators waited impatiently for the winner to finish off his rival and bag his victory. When nothing of that sort happened for a long time and the organisers told the winner to slay the opponent, the winner looked up, cast his glances all around, looked into face of the king that enjoyed the fight, lifted off his sword and threw the sword towards the king. The sword darted off with lightning speed and slashed neck of the king. In no time, the slain king fell in his chair, dead.

The organisers, spectators and royal guards were shocked with gory happening of something that they never imagined. Pin drop silence made place in the court for some time. Very soon, the royal guards surrounded killer of the king and the killer surrendered to them, with no resistance whatsoever. The commander of the guards said to the killer:

"Why did you commit the dastardly act?"

"To put a stop to an ugly game that is costing lives of many fighters," said the fighter.

"You will be killed for this atrocity," said the guard.

"I am prepared," said the fighter.

Suddenly, a wave of applause in adoration of the fighter-killer started among the armed soldiers and, for fear of backlash from them, the elite onlookers fled fast from their places. The fighter-killer eventually seized the throne and became a king. He promulgated orders for playing game as a game and removed killing from it. He ruled the kingdom kindly and humanely.

88. THE FALL

A man renounced worldly life and embraced divine life at a very young age. He went into forest, spent solitary life for a long time and performed austere penance in propitiation of god. He realized god at last. He decided to spread message of god among worldly people, left the forest and went on a long mission. He went around from place to place, met many people on the way, took part in religious gatherings and delivered speeches on virtues of otherworldly life. His teaching and preaching appealed to public and drew large crowds. He wrote a few literary works on divine matters. The works drew admiration from learned litterateurs. The man, at a very young age, became a celebrity and commanded respect from wherever he went. He never stayed at one place. He wandered all the time, all over the places, wherever his legs could take him to.

One day, the saint headed towards a town. He reached a river, on other side of which the town lay, and he waited for someone to ferry him across the river by a boat. He found none nearby. He looked around. He saw at a distance a palatial house, situated in the midst of a sprawling garden on a mound, dotted with high rise trees and enclosed all around. He went to the palace to see if he could find someone, who could transport him across the river. He saw there a charming lady, sitting under shade of a tree in front yard of the house. At sight of him, the lady rose up at once, approached him, took him respectfully inside the palace and said:

"I am gratified to have your presence in my house."

"Who are you?" said the saint.

"I am a courtesan," said the courtesan.

"I want help from you," said the saint.

"Bid me," said the courtesan.

"I am to go to other side of the river. Can you arrange someone, who can take me across the stream?" said the saint.

"You will not find any one to help you at this time of evening. Be pleased to stay here for the night. I shall arrange for your journey tomorrow," said the courtesan.

"As you say," said the saint.

The next day for the saint to cross the stream did not dawn. The saint fell to charms of the courtesan. He embraced a new way of life and stayed on with the courtesan.

Many years passed. The saint turned old. One day, he happened to cross the river and go to the town, which he wanted to go to, long ago, on some errand. He heard that there was a big religious congregation in the town hall. He went to the hall, packed with public. He managed to find place to stand in one corner of the hall and waited for the function to start.

When the function started, many speakers in a row spoke eloquently on greatness of a saint, who contributed immensely to spreading splendour of divinity among people and brought a big change in their way of life. The saint stood there all through the show and, after end of the show, went back home. He did not like to call back to memory what the speakers spoke about in the function, since the speakers spoke about none other than him.

89. HALF MARK

A student stood first in his school, in school final examination. He scored very good marks. Based on his merit, he secured a seat, in a technical course in a college in a far off city. He was very happy. He joined the course. He stayed in a hostel attached to the college.

By nature, the student was highly diligent, disciplined and study minded. But staying independently in hostel, coming in contact with new friends and exposure to city environment brought a big change in him. The student was completely changed. He neglected studies, took to whiling away time in the company of friends that did not bother to study and wasted his whole academic year.

He woke up and realized his mistake, only when his first year drew to a close and annual examinations were round the corner. He became highly panicky. With fear of examinations haunting him and left with very little time for preparation, he shuddered to think how he could write his examinations well. He cursed himself for his negligence and foolhardiness. However, he applied himself to studies in the last minute, studied seriously whatever he could study within a short span of time that was available with him, and wrote the examinations. He fared badly in the examinations. He reviewed his performance and guessed that he would just scrape though all subjects, excepting one, and he was most likely to fail in that one subject. The very thought of failure created in him tremors. He knew very well that in case he failed, he would be constrained to repeat his first year, since there was no provision for automatic promotion to the next year, as per rules of the course that he pursued. He turned highly nervous. He could not even bear the thought of detention in first year.

He waited restlessly for two months for his first year examination results to come out. He saw hell on earth during the two months. With the shadow of failure hovering above him, he spent sleepless nights. He had dreams and saw in his dreams that he failed and continued his first year for the second time. He lost weight and peace of mind. He became sickly.

At last, the D day came. The results were out. The student came to know that the results were available in office of head of department of his branch. He ran to the office. A faculty member there read out results, hall ticket number wise. The student stood there impatiently and waited for his result being announced. He passed through a strange situation. He reeled under tremendous pressure. He quivered from head to foot. He felt as though the ground underneath his feet melted away. He feared that he could swoon any time. His heart palpitated very fast. His eyes and ears remained firmly turned on the announcer. And finally the announcement came. The student passed. He was relieved. He yelled in joy. He went to the announcer, confirmed his pass once again and left the office. He felt as if a great load on his head got removed all of a sudden and he became very free.

Next day, he went to the office again and collected his marks memorandum. As he expected, he secured just a few marks above minimum pass marks in all subjects excepting the one, in which he fared the worst. He looked for marks that he secured in that subject. He secured thirty four and half marks and the marks were rounded off to thirty five, the minimum for pass in a subject. The student was flabbergasted. He thanked his stars that favoured him. He thanked the evaluator that gave him thirty four and half marks. He thanked the system of evaluation that provided for rounding off half mark to full mark.

The nerve breaking experience taught the student a big lesson. The student felt as if someone gave a slap on his cheek and pulled him out of a dangerous situation that he was caught in. He sincerely repented for his folly and took a firm resolve not to face a situation that he faced again in his life. He was wholly transformed. He became his own old self. He left the friends, in whose company he ruined his first year, got back into serious studies again and made amends for what he lost in his first year. He passed his final year with flying colours and secured a job, soon after going out of the college.

90. GRATITUDE

There lived a learned man in a town. He hailed from a family of scholars. He read scriptures, mythologies and works of great authors. Most of the time, he lived with only reading and writing. Other than that, he did nothing at home. His wife was a good home manager. She took complete care of home affairs. But she was a lady of different stuff. She did not approve of what her husband did. Many a time, she coaxed and coerced her husband to come out of what he did and pay attention to doing something for earning livelihood. But the learned man did not heed his wife. He remained in his own world. Over a period of time, the wife got highly jittery with attitude of her husband and poured out her anger on him. The learned man did not react. He received what his wife said in silence and never reacted.

Many uneventful years passed. The learned man remained what he was and his wife remained what she was. Both remained under one roof with the wife venting out her strong feelings of disapproval and the learned man receiving them most compliantly.

One fine day, the learned man received invitation from king of the land to participate in a literary meet in the state capital. The learned man went to the state capital along with his better half. He participated in the meet and became a cynosure among participants for erudite knowledge that he possessed. The king was highly impressed with works of the scholar. He hid no feelings to express his appreciation for the scholar. He publicly praised the learned man for the extraordinary knowledge that he possessed and some of the great works that he penned. He said to the scholar:

"Your contribution to literature is unparalleled. I do not know how you could write such great and voluminous works. I really want to know how you could do such a feat and what is the secret behind your success?"

"My wife," said the scholar, unhesitatingly.

"What do you mean?" said the king.

"Secret of my success is my wife. She sacrificed her entire life to support me. She earned bread for me. She managed house for me. She burnt like a candle to give me light. If I have done something, it is only due to my wife," said the scholar.

The king was highly pleased with frank admission by the scholar. He honoured both the scholar and his wife and showered riches on them.

91. INTERVIEW

A candidate appeared for interview before a panel of interviewers. The interviewers, one after another, put many questions to the candidate and got no proper answers from him. They concluded that the candidate did not answer the questions well and he did not qualify for the selection. At end of the interview, one of the interviewers went through the resume put up by the candidate and remarked:

"Based on what you wrote in your resume, we have thought that you can do very well in the interview. But we are sorry to say that your interview performance is not in matching with your academic performance."

"I admit with humility, sir," said the interviewee.

"Now, you may go," said the interviewer.

"Thank you for the opportunity you gave me for interview, today. Before I leave, I wish to say something. May I request you to give me permission to do so," said the interviewee.

"Please say," said the interviewer.

"You have remarked that I did not do well in the interview and my performance in interview is not in keeping with my academic record," said the interviewee.

"Yes, our observation is right," said the interviewer.

"Sir, I am a novice. I am fresh from college. I know only what is taught in our curriculum. You may find fault with me, if you ask me questions from the subjects that I studied and I fail to answer them. How far is it right to put questions from practical field in which I don't have any experience and prove that my performance is bad," said the candidate getting up and preparing to leave the interview chamber.

What the candidate said appealed to chairman of the committee. He smiled, gesticulated to the candidate to sit back and made one of the interviewers in the committee to shower questions, picked up from subjects taught in college, on the aspirant. The job aspirant answered the questions perfectly well. He got selected. While exiting, the candidate thanked the committee and the committee thanked the candidate.

92. NOT DOING ANYTHING

A noble was vexed with his son, who did nothing. He tried in many ways to mend his son. But his son did not change. The noble was at a loss to understand how to change his son for good. He went to a learned friend to take his advice on the subject. He said to his learned friend:

"I want your help."

"Tell me, how I can help you?" said the learned friend.

"My son is idle. He is doing nothing. He is not showing interest in doing any work," said the noble.

"I don't believe what you say," said the learned friend.

"Why do you disbelieve me?" said the noble.

"In my opinion, there can be none in the world, who wants to sit idly, doing nothing," said the learned friend.

"But my son is doing it," said the noble.

"How do you say so?" said the learned friend.

"He is not doing anything that I am asking him to do," said the noble.

"He may not be doing what you are asking him to do. But he may be interested to do what he wants to do," said the learned friend.

"What shall I do?" said the noble.

"Allow your son to do what he wants. His idleness will vanish," said the learned friend.

The noble followed advice of his learned friend. His son shed his idleness.

93. MIGRAINE

A student developed migraine. He suffered severely from it. He went to many doctors. But medicines given by no doctor worked. Under effect of migraine, the student writhed with unbearable pain. One day, a visitor that came to his house suggested to the student to go to an old woman, who was grandmother of a cattle breeder, and who had a wonderful drug for migraine. The student went at once to house of the cattle breeder, met the old lady and told her his problem. The old lady checked up the place, where the student complained of pain, went inside the house, brought two green leaves, wrung them between her palms until they became wet with dark green fluid oozing out of them, put the crushed leaves near nose of the student and asked the student to smell the leaves that emitted strong odour. The student smelt the leaves and felt relieved. He offered to pay something to the old lady. But the lady refused to take anything. The student thanked the lady and went away. The drug worked so well that the student got cured of his problem once for all and he never developed migraine thereafter.

In later years, the student pursued medical studies and became a doctor. He remembered how he suffered from migraine in his earlier days and how the old lady cured him of the pain. He noticed that there was no effective medicine for migraine in the school of medicine that he studied. He wanted to learn the art of curing migraine from the old lady. He went to the old lady. But he was informed that the old lady passed away long ago. He asked son of the old lady:

"I am feeling very sorry to hear that the old lady passed away. I came here to learn the art of curing migraine from her. I shall be very happy, if anyone of you in the family can teach me the technique."

"We are very sorry. We can't help you," said the cattle breeder.

"Why?" said the doctor.

"My mother offered to teach us the technique, many a time. But we showed no interest. Secret of the technique is buried along with my mother," said the cattle breeder.

The doctor felt very sorry to note that a great treatment that came down to the old lady from her predecessors got buried with her permanently.

94. SUPER-DELEGATION

A new General Manager took over reigns of a factory from his predecessor. He was highly sociable. He spent most of his time in talking to people that mattered most to him. He spoke to departmental heads regularly, received visitors that called on him, interacted with his higher ups from time to time, took care of requirements of his customers and held scheduled meetings with heads of representative bodies in office in the factory. He was always in his cabin. He wore always a relaxed look and a winning smile on his face. Employees in the factory, who knew how hard the predecessor worked to extract production from the factory, wondered at relaxed way of working of the new head and doubted if at all he could manage the factory. One day, the head of a representative body met the General Manager and said to him:

"Sir, I have a doubt. May I ask?"

"Please ask," said the General Manager.

"You are always in your cabin. Is it not necessary for you to visit shop floors to know what is happening there?" said the representative.

"No," said the General Manager.

The representative was stunned. He looked blankly into face of the General Manager. The General Manager answered further to clarify doubt of the representative. He said:

"If I start going to shop floors to monitor what is happening there, I shall be doing the job what my officers in the shop floors are supposed to do and my officers working there will stop working. I don't want my officers down below to stop working and super delegate their work to me."

The representative appreciated logic of the General Manager. In later days, the General Manager proved his standpoint right and succeeded very well in his work management.

95. MORE CORRUPT

There worked an employee in an organisation. He was a free advice giver. He never stayed in his place. He never bothered to do any job assigned to him. He was always on his move. He met departmental heads and gave them his unsolicited opinions on how to do work, how to take care of workers, how managements in foreign countries treated their employees, what he read in various books and how working conditions were to be improved. He posed as if he was a very knowledgeable man and tried to get close to the head, whom he met. Some departmental heads heard him and nodded their heads to what he said. Some other heads heard him and simply ignored what he said. Over the years, the free adviser did nothing other than roaming around on a self created mission of giving advices to others.

One day, a local news paper published news on corruption rampant in the organisation. The free advisor was concerned. He decided to talk to head of the organisation on the issue. He sought interview with the head. The head granted it. The free adviser met the head and said:

"Sir, have you seen a report on corruption in our organisation in today's newspaper."

"I saw it," said the head.

"I am feeling highly concerned about the report," said the free adviser.

"I too am feeling very sad about the state of affairs prevailing in the organisation," said the head.

"Sir, you must take action against the people who are corrupt," said the free adviser.

"That I am not able to take," said the head.

"Why sir," said the free adviser.

"If I have to take action against people who are corrupt, I must take action against people, who are more corrupt," said the head.

"Who are more corrupt?" said the free adviser.

"People who are not sticking to their seats, not doing what they are supposed to do and wandering around like vagabonds," said the head.

The free advisor suddenly got up, excused himself and exited instantly from office of the head.

96. POLITICAL RIVAL

Candidates, fielded by two political parties, fought an election, for the post of mayor of a big city. Candidate of the first political party won the election and became mayor of the city. He was a man of great vision and high mission. He strived hard to serve the citizens that elected him. He unleashed many new schemes to improve water supply, power supply, drainage system, public transport, hygiene, educational facilities, parks, play grounds, streets, street lights, safety, security and other amenities for better living in the city. He took steps to protect water bodies and public properties in the city. He went for construction of schools, theatrical houses and hospitals in various parts of the city. He facilitated establishment of industrial corridors in suburbs of the city. He catalysed municipal administration to take services to door steps of city dwellers, address their grievances, take their opinion for better governance and make them active partners in overall development of the city. He made a lot to improve lot of the common man. He made his presence felt by public through his path breaking and proactive actions. He received all out appreciation for his action packed rule, from one and all.

On one side, the mayor unleashed many schemes for wellbeing of his people. On the other side, he established a firm grip on his administration. He awarded employees that worked hard. He punished employees that worked hardly. He mercilessly weeded out corrupt employees from their places. He became a terror for law breakers, land grabbers, nuisance creators, trouble makers, fraudsters, illegal money spinners and other wrong doers, who posed a potential threat to peace in city. He became intolerant to people in his own party, who erred. Because of his uncompromising attitude, over a period of time, many people belonging to his own party turned against him. Dissent simmered and resentment reached a flashpoint within his party circles. Some disgruntled elements in the party openly waged a war against the mayor and made preparations to overthrow him.

With dissent simmering in ruling party against the mayor, people in the rival party got jubilant. They approached their defeated leader and said to him:

"The mayor is facing serious problem within his party. This is the best time for us to act. Let us search for ways to find fault with the mayor and make him unpopular."

"The mayor is doing a wonderful job. It is not correct on our part to criticize him," said leader of the rival political party.

"Members of the ruling party are up in arms over uncompromising attitude of the mayor. There is nothing wrong, if we criticize," said members of the rival political party.

"I am not a member of the ruling party. I cannot stoop down to level of the ruling party members," said leader of the rival political party.

Members of the rival party withdrew from their attempt. The mayor continued until his tenure was over and stepped down. He did not fight the election a second time. Instead, he supported the rival leader wholeheartedly and saw that he was elected mayor.

97. FULL LIST

A brilliant engineer worked hard, climbed up ladder of his professional career very fast and reached the top of the tree. He became CEO of a giant organisation. Representatives of various associations of employees working in the organisation met the CEO, congratulated him for elevation to the coveted post and pledged their support to the CEO.

A representative, belonging to a community to which the CEO belonged, met the CEO and submitted a list to the CEO. The CEO glanced through the list and said:

"What is this list?"

"This is the list our people in the organisation," said the representative.

"Why are you giving me this list?" said the CEO.

"With a view that you will help our people," said the representative.

"But why are you giving me part of the list. This is not the full list," said the CEO.

"This is the full list," argued the representative.

"Sorry, this is not the full list. Full list is with me. I don't mind giving a copy of the full list to you," said the CEO, handing over to the representative, complete list of all employees working in the organisation.

98. SATISFACTION

A student pursued engineering studies in a college. He was good at studies of his core engineering subjects. He was equally good at studies of language related subjects. He enthusiastically participated in many literary activities. He took part in essay writing and elocution competitions both at collegiate as well as inter-collegiate level and earned several prizes. Because of his deep interest in English language and activities related to it, he happened to become very close to a lecturer, who taught English in the college.

The student completed his course in the college, attended to final examinations, left the college for the last and went back to his native place. In the examination results declared after three months, the student stood second in the college. When he went to college for collection of his college leaving certificates, he met the English lecturer and told him happily about the result. The English lecturer apparently was not very happy. He said disapprovingly:

"I am not happy with you."

"What happened, sir?" said the student.

"How many marks did the first ranker get more than what you got?" said the lecturer.

"Just two marks," said the student.

"In which subjects did he get more marks?" said the lecturer.

"In sessional marks of two subjects, awarded by internal faculty of college," said the student.

"And you secured marks higher than what the first ranker got in all external evaluations," said the lecturer.

"Yes, sir," said the student.

"Don't you know that I am very close to Head of Department of your discipline?" said the lecturer.

"I know, sir," said the student.

"I really don't know that you are very bright in your engineering subjects too. Had I known it beforehand, I could have asked your Head to give you better internal marks, such that you could have stood first in the college. I am feeling very sorry, you didn't avail of my help," said the lecturer.

"Thank you for your concern, sir. But I am not feeling sorry," said the student.

"Why do you say so?" said the lecturer.

"Had I got the first rank with your influence, I would not have felt as happy as I am feeling now. Had I become first with your influence, it would have smitten my conscience forever that I got my first only because of you. Now, even though I am second in college, I am feeling very elated, because what I got is out of my own effort," said the student.

99. LAW AND ORDER

Under the rule of an elected head, law and order situation in a nation deteriorated very badly. The society turned into a sizzling volcano. It became turbulent and troubled.

It disintegrated into splinters. Various social groups making up the society separated out from one another and fought pitched battles openly in streets. Groupings, gatherings, hate speeches, stabbings, lootings, squabbling, sloganeering and rallying became affair of everyday. Bloodshed became very common. Rumour mongers and disinformation campaigners were on their unchecked spree. Young and old behaved alike. They left law of land to winds and moved about with sticks and swords in their hands. Worst of all was, the unruly mobs worked under guidance of rival leaders of the ruling party. The common men, who had no political affiliation, the poor and the people, who lived on their daily wages, lost their means of livelihood and suffered the worst.

The law enforcement machinery remained paralysed. The authorities handling law and order could do nothing. They stood like mute spectators, unable to take action, since the warring groups had blessings of some of the ruling party members. The law and order totally went out of control of the law enforcers.

In the elections that followed, the ruling party lost election out to an opposition party. The elected head of the party that won elections took the place of the old head. The new head checked effectively unruliness in the society and brought law and order situation under control, within no time. Many people, who never expected that things could change for better in society of the kingdom in immediate future, wondered how the new head did a wonder, practically within no time. A battery of news reporters met the new elected head of the government, congratulated him for his success in controlling law and order situation in the nation and said:

"How could you check unruliness in society that ruled the roost for a long time?"

"I gave free hand to my administration to act," said the new head.

100. ELIXIR

One day, when a king was in his court hall, a guard came and announced that a young man wanted to see the king. The king permitted. The guard withdrew. A young man entered the court hall, made his obeisance to the king and said:

"Oh king, I came for your help."

"Who are you and what help do you seek from me?" said the king.

"I am the son of a medical practitioner. My father is well versed in preparation of medicines from medicinal plants. During his lifelong practice, he found out that certain plants hold secrets for increasing longevity of life. He extensively studied medicinal values of the plants and developed fascination to prepare an elixir that increases longevity of life from them. But, before he hit his invention, he passed away. I want to continue the research from where my father left. I want help from you for the research project," said the researcher.

"What type of help do you want?" said the king.

"I want food, shelter and facilities for research," said the researcher.

"I grant what you want," said the king.

Arrangements were made for comfortable stay of the researcher and all facilities required for research were made available to him. The researcher started off with his research. The project continued for years on end. When the researcher failed to produce the elixir even after five years, many courtiers in service of the king started talking among themselves that the researcher was wasting royal funds for no useful end. The murmurings reached the king. The king called the researcher one day and said to him in presence of some of his high placed courtiers:

"How far has your research come up to, for production of elixir?"

"Your Majesty, I am yet to make a breakthrough," said the researcher.

"I am losing confidence in you," said the king.

"If Your Majesty is not pleased with my work, I shall stop my research forthwith," said the researcher.

"Don't do it. Please continue it," said the king.

The researcher left the place. Every one present with the king was astonished with queer decision of the king. The king looked at his courtiers, read their feelings and said:

"The researcher has failed to produce the elixir that he wanted to produce. But he produced a wonderful medicine for a disease that mankind has been suffering from, with no proper treatment for it, for a long time," said the king.

"I beg to say something, in this context," said one courtier.

"Please speak out," said the king.

"I am told that the researcher has stumbled upon his invention by chance," said the courtier.

"Most of the inventions have come into light, only by chance. It is very common in the field of research that what is envisaged is not hit upon and what is most unexpected is invented. We may not be able to attribute what is hit upon by accident to direct success of research. But hitting upon by accident is not possible, without a researcher researching for what he wants to invent. What is invented may not be as significant as what is sought after. But that too is great from a different point of view. That is the reason why I permitted the researcher to continue his research. He may or may not produce the elixir that he is working on. But, I am sure, more accidental inventions will come out of his research," said the king.

The courtiers praised merit in logic of their learned king.

101. GOOD DAYS

A young man felt that he was haunted by ill luck. He recollected that he passed through a bad period, at every point of time in his past. He had a doubt whether he was lucky to have good days in his life or not. He wanted to know about it from a learned man. He heard that there was a diviner in a forest and he predicted very precisely when good days would start in the life of someone. He went to the diviner and said:

"When will good days start in my life?"

"What did you do for good days to start in your life?" said the diviner.

"I waited for good days to start in my life," said the young man.

"Good days will never come for you in your life time," said the diviner.

"Why do you say so?" said the young man.

"Good days are those that come with fruits for your past deeds. If you did nothing in the past, how do you expect good days to come for you in your life?" said the diviner.

The young man understood real meaning of good days and got seriously into doing something concretely. Very soon, good days paraded before him, with baskets of benefits on their heads that resulted out of his good deeds.

102. LEARNING

A young man belonged to a backward village, where all villagers were illiterate. By sheer stroke of luck, he got a chance to get literate. He cradled a desire to learn more. He left his village, went to a nearby town, learnt more and became very learned. A desire made place in him to make all people of his village literate. He went back to his village, met headman of the village and expressed what was there in his mind. The headman appreciated noble thought of the young man and encouraged him to do what he desired to do. The young man started a free school in his house, went to every house in the village and told the householders to send their children to school. Every householder lauded the young man. But no one volunteered to send his wards to the school. Very few students joined the school. The young man turned very unhappy with attitude of the villagers. He compromised with teaching handful of the students that joined his school.

A few years passed. The young man entered middle age. The feeling, that his planned mission to spread literacy in the village fell through, pricked him. The dejected teacher felt for sure that the village did not want his services and there was no purpose for him to run the school in the village, any more. He decided to close down the school and move away to the town, where he was educated.

All of a sudden, a big change came over the village. A group of villagers met the teacher and informed him that they wanted to send all their children to his school. Besides, they took a piece of land, constructed a school on it and requested the teacher to run the school in the newly constructed premises. The teacher was very happy. He dropped the idea of closing down the school and shifted the school from his home to the new place. Children from the village joined the new school in large numbers.

The young man did not understand why such a sudden change came over the villagers. One day, he talked to one of the villagers to clarify his doubt:

"Many years ago, when I started the school and requested the villagers to send their children to school, no one volunteered. When I am about to close down the school, many villagers sent their children. Why such a sudden change came over the villagers?"

"Years ago, you wanted us to learn. Now we want to learn," said the villager.

103. DESIRE FOR MORE

There lived a jackal in a forest. He starved for food. He set out in a dark night in search of a prey. He chanced upon none. He heard a suppressed roar. He went in direction of the sound and saw a tiger that ate a goat that it killed. He waited until the tiger went away, moved to where remains of the hunted animal were there, held in his mouth a fleshy leg of the slain goat and moved away to a safe hideout to feast on its prized find. He was happy, because he found something for a brunch.

On way, he found a rabbit fast asleep at the base of a tree. He could not resist his temptation for the rabbit. He left the leg piece in a safe place, walked silently towards the rabbit and fell upon it. The rabbit was too quick to fall a prey. It woke up in the last minute and ran away. The jackal was disappointed. He cursed his ill luck and returned to pick up what he left. The leg piece was no more there.

104. DISAPPOINTMENT

A young merchant, in his late teens, desired to be recognised as the shrewdest, by people known to him in his town. He tried to do many kinds of business, amass wealth and get the recognition that he craved for. But his trials did not bear fruit. The merchant decided to leave the town, go to foreign lands and try his luck. His parents, friends and relatives persuaded the young man not to leave the town and go to unknown lands. But the persuasions did not yield results. The merchant left his family members, everyone known to him and left the town to lands, where he could make a fortune.

The merchant went far away to foreign lands. He worked relentlessly. He succeeded in his businesses. He accumulated wealth far more than what he targeted for. After end of his business mission, he wound up his businesses and returned happily to his home town. He set foot on his birth place with a fond hope that his family members, friends, relatives, neighbours and acquaintances would meet him and rain recognition on him for his amazing and trailblazing success. He met with disappointment. Nothing of what he expected happened.

When the merchant wondered for what happened and tried to find reason for how such a thing happened, he came to know that all those that he desired to meet and get recognition from passed away long ago. The merchant returned home after more than fifty years, when he turned sufficiently old.

105. SALE STRATEGY

A householder sat in portico of his house and pored over a morning newspaper, leisurely. A young man in the street greeted the householder from outside of compound wall of the house and said:

"Sir, may I take two minutes of your time."

"What is the matter?" said the householder, getting up from his seat and seeing the young man standing in the street.

"I am from office of a local newspaper. May I request you to take our newspaper," said the young man.

"I am in no need of it. I am already getting an English newspaper," said the householder.

"Ours is a newspaper in local language. It covers all local news. Please take it," said the young man.

"I am not finding time to go through one newspaper. What shall I do with another newspaper?" said the householder.

"Be pleased to take the paper, sir. If I don't promote the paper, I may lose my job," said the young man.

"Sorry, young man! I don't want it," said the householder.

"Take at least for one month, sir. Later on, if you want to stop the paper, you may do it," said the young man.

"OK," said the householder, reluctantly.

The salesman took down address and other details of the householder, thanked him for his good gesture and went away. The local newspaper started coming to house of the householder from starting of the next day.

The householder wanted to stop the newspaper after one month. But that one month never came. The householder continued to receive the newspaper month after month. After a few months, he got adjusted to receiving two papers in his house.

106. DOCTOR'S WORD

One morning, a man got out of bed and felt that he had pain in his shoulder. He wondered why the pain developed, all of a sudden. He shrugged it off, by thinking that it could be some muscle pain and it would subside very soon. But when the pain persisted even after a month, the man decided not to take any risk and consulted a doctor. The doctor examined the man, conducted some medical tests and confirmed that there was nothing to worry about and nothing was seriously wrong. He prescribed a pain balm to be applied externally on the shoulder and a few pain killers to be used only in case of severe pain. The man thanked the doctor, went home and told his wife what the doctor said. When his wife volunteered to apply the balm, the man refused. The wife was astonished. She said:

"Why are you refusing the balm?"

"I don't need it," said the man.

"Why do you say so?" said wife of the man.

"My pain is gone," said the man.

"You didn't even apply the balm. How is the pain gone?" said wife of the man.

"Doctor's words that I don't have any serious problem to worry about have cured me of my pain," said the man.

The wife understood that her husband doubted in his mind that there could be some serious problem for his pain and the pain persisted because of the doubt. She mused that the doctor's words removed the doubt and pain was gone with it.

107. TRANSFER TO HOME STATE

A big company had many divisions spread throughout length and breadth of a country. An employee, working in one of the divisions, wanted to have a transfer to the division, which was located in his home state. He went to head of the division, where he worked, and said to him:

"Sir, I want a transfer to the division located in my home state."

"Are you sure that you will be happy there?" said the head.

"I am sure I shall be very happy," said the employee.

"Well, I shall transfer you," said the head.

The employee, after a few weeks, got his transfer to the division of his choice. He was very happy. He shifted to the place, where he was transferred. Within a very short time, he approached head of the new division and said:

"I request you to transfer me back to the division, wherefrom I have come."

"You came here on transfer, very recently. Why do you want to go back again?" said head of the new division.

"I was more comfortable in the division from which I came," said the employee.

"Why do you say so?" said head of the new division.

"When I was in my previous division, I belonged to a very big group, representing people from my state. Before opting for a transfer here, I thought I was coming to my home state, where a bigger group representing people from my state worked," said the employee.

"Now?" said head of the new division.

"After coming here, I have realized that I have not become member of a bigger group representing people from my state, but micro groups that exist in the name of caste, town, district and other specifics. I am feeling suffocated to be under the umbrellas of smaller groups," said the employee.

Request of the employee was heard. The employee got his transfer. He went back very happily to the division, from which he came earlier.

108. GOODWILL

In good olden days, there ruled a kingdom, democratically elected rulers. Once in a period of time, a high level statute body of the kingdom conducted elections and whosoever won the election became ruler of the land. The aspirants of power, who fought elections to become rulers, went into general public, with manifesto of what they intended to do, in case they were elected to power. In the process of seeking mandate of the public, the contestants wooed voters with distribution of money, food, clothing, liquor and what the public wanted. The contestants, once elected to power, ruled unethically, usurped public funds, amassed wealth and defended themselves with the argument that the ill gotten money was required to fight the next elections. With the rulers patronising corruption, corruption became a way of life in the royal establishment. Ruler after ruler did the same.

Once, a young ruler, who earnestly desired to bring a change in the lives of people in the kingdom, went aggressively for campaigning into public, spent nothing to woo the voters, convinced the voters that he would extend an ideal rule and won the election. He became ruler of the land.

Counsellors in the royal establishment advised the king to amass money, as the erstwhile rulers did. The king was surprised. He said to them:

"Why are you advising me to amass money?"

"Unless you do it, you will not have money to fight the next elections," said the counsellors.

"I don't want money to fight the next election," said the ruler.

"How will you fight the next election without money?" said the counsellors.

"With goodwill that I earn out of my rule," said the ruler.

109. TURNING AWAY

A little boy wanted a chocolate. He pestered his mother to give him money for the chocolate. His mother gave him a ten rupee note. The boy went to a nearby shop, gave the note to the shop keeper and asked him to give him a one rupee chocolate. The shop keeper took the note, gave the boy the chocolate and did not return the change. The boy waited for the change. But the shop keeper turned to other customers and started attending to their needs. The boy waited for some time and asked the shop keeper for the change. The shop keeper looked at the boy differently and said:

"What change are you asking for?"

"I gave you a ten rupee note. You gave me a chocolate for one rupee. You have to return nine rupees," said the boy.

"Don't tell me. You gave me one rupee and I gave you chocolate for it. Don't lie. Go," said the shop keeper.

The boy got offended. He felt ashamed in presence of other customers standing before the shop. He lowered his head. He had tears welling up in his eyes. He could do nothing to take change from the shop keeper. He went back home very unhappily. He went with a resolve never to visit the shop again. And further to it, true to his resolve, he, in his life time, never went to the shop again to buy anything.

110. GOD

A king did not believe in god. He held the view that concept of god was only a figment of imagination. He argued vehemently that god was not there and it was unwise to worship god. Considering the coveted position he held, no one challenged his viewpoint. But many people in their hearts felt that the king was not right in challenging existence of god. Some courtiers close to the king tried to convince him that god was there. But the king did not agree. The king made it clear that he would believe in god, only if someone showed the god in his physical form. He also announced big prize money for whosoever showed him god.

Announcement of prize money tempted many. Many people tried in many ways to convince the king that god existed. Some showed god in the form of idols in shrines. Some showed the god in the form of trees, hills, rivers, stars and other holy objects in nature. Some showed the god in the form of living and bygone persons that rendered great service to humanity. But, all of them failed in their efforts to make the king believe in existence of god. When virtually every one gave up, a little girl came forward to show god to the king. The king was amused. He went with the little girl inside a cave shrine, saw the god there, shown by the girl, emerged out of the cave, beaming with immense happiness, and said to his courtiers that waited outside the cave:

"I have seen the god."

The courtiers were surprised. They asked the girl how she showed the god. The girl said nothing and smiled in reply. The prize money was given away to the girl. For a long time, the girl did not disclose what she showed to the king. One day, when she was in a very happy mood and her mother asked her to reveal what she showed to the king, the girl said:

"I showed god to our king in the form of his own image in a mirror."

111. PHOTO

An employee worked in department of a factory for more than three decades. All throughout his service, every day, he worshipped a goddess, the framed photo of which was there in the department. He immensely liked imposing multi colour image of the framed photo. He had a feeling that the goddess showered on him her benediction.

The employee attained the age of superannuation. On the last day of his service in the department, subordinates of the employee collected all his personal belongings and kept them ready to be sent with him. A junior colleague of the employee said to him:

"Sir, we have collected all your belongings. Please have a look. In case anything more is left, we shall pack them."

"Do one thing. I want a photo of the goddess in our department. Please take it. I shall have it with me as a token of remembrance," said the employee.

"We shall do it," said the junior colleague.

At end of the day, the employee left the department in which he worked all his life, exited out from main gate of the factory and went home. His colleagues brought behind him all his personal belongings and kept them in his house.

Next day, the retiree looked at the personal belongings, brought from his office. While going through them, he saw a big packet, covered with a newspaper. He didn't understand what it was. He opened the packet. He was wonder struck. From the packet, came out framed photo of the goddess that he worshipped all throughout his life and for whom he developed high reverence. The retiree gave a ring to his junior colleague and said:

"By mistake, you sent with my belongings photo of the goddess in our department."

"Sir, you wanted the photo and I sent it," said the junior colleague.

"I said I wanted a photo of the photo," said the retiree.

"I mistook it to be photo of the goddess," said the junior colleague.

The man wondered how photo of the goddess that he worshipped, came by mistake to his house. He put photo of the goddess in prayer place of his house and continued to offer prayers to the goddess, as he did in his office. He took it for granted that the goddess entered his house as a sign of benediction and he was sure to be crowned with success in his retired phase of life. With the belief acting strongly at back of his mind, he tried for success and got it in abundance.

112. THREE POINT FORMULA

A mathematician turned a mentor. He postulated a three-point-formula for achievement of success in life and elaborated on the same to customers that came to consult him. He satisfied the customers with his mathematical logic, mixed with mentoring talent.

One day, a budding mentor, who practised a two-point-formula for achievement of success in life, met the senior mentor, introduced himself and said:

"I know about two point formula. I don't know about three point formula. I request you to explain it to me."

"Tell me about your two point formula. I shall explain to you later, about my three point formula," said the senior mentor.

"We must know where we were yesterday and where are we today. If we join the two points, we come to know whether we are on right track in life or not. My two point theory is precisely that," said the junior mentor.

"As you feel, two points are sufficient to draw a straight line. But the straight line drawn with two points cannot determine whether we are on right track in life or not. One more point is required to determine that," said the senior mentor.

"What is the third point?" said the junior mentor.

"The point where we should be tomorrow," said the senior mentor.

"How will it help?" said the junior mentor.

"The straight line joining the point where we were yesterday and the point where we shall be tomorrow will determine where should be the point of where we are today. That tells where we are and where we should be and it guides us on what correction we should make to fall in the straight line," said the senior mentor.

The junior mentor thanked the senior mentor for his advanced theorem on success in life and changed over to practising the new concept.

113. SICKNESS

An accountant was very hale and healthy. He never had any health related problems. He retired from service. He spent time happily at home. All of a sudden, he fell ill. He went to a doctor. The doctor checked up general health condition of the accountant and certified that he had no problem. The accountant was not satisfied. He went to a second doctor. The second doctor too endorsed opinion of the first doctor. The accountant was annoyed. He expressed unhappily that the doctors did not treat him well. Wife of the accountant was at a loss to understand what to do. She took the accountant to a specialist. The specialist too went with opinion of the previous doctors. The accountant grew disenchanted with the medical profession. He spent time at home cursing his ill luck. Day by day, his health deteriorated.

The wife thought and got a bright idea. She went to a relative, who ran a shop in a market place and told him something. The relative wondered, but agreed to do what the lady said. He went to house of the lady and said to the retired accountant:

"I am told that you are very good at accounting work. If you are free at home and you like, will you please come and help me in accounting work in my shop."

"What can I do? I am not doing well," said the accountant.

"Come at least for a couple of hours. It will be a great relief for me. My man will come and pick you up daily," said the shop keeper.

The accountant obliged request of the shop keeper. The shop keeper treated the accountant well. Instead of spending a couple of hours in the shop, the accountant started spending complete day in the shop. He forgot that he was sick.

114. ADDICTION

A school going child was addicted to internet. He spent most of the time with playing games, watching videos and doing something or other on the net. He was so deeply immersed in the net that he hardly played games or moved with friends. His parents were worried. They tried to peel the child off the net. But they failed. They took the child to a psychologist. The psychologist heard what the parents said, studied behaviour of the child and, after analysis, suggested:

"Your child is highly addicted to the net. Do everything possible to keep the child engaged in some or other physical activity and keep him off from the net."

"That we are not able to do," said the parents.

"Why do you say so?" said the psychologist.

"Both of us are employed. We cannot afford to sit with the child and make him change his habit," said the parents.

"If that is the case, there is only one solution," said the psychologist.

"What is it?" said the parents.

"Live with the problem," said the psychologist.

115. TRANSFERS

A businessman owned a factory that manufactured engineering goods. He wanted to double production in the factory. But experts indicated that capacity availability in the factory was insufficient to take additional load. The businessman set up a second factory, away from the first factory. He called head of the first factory and said:

"Please select some good people and transfer them to the second factory."

The head of the first factory got an opportunity to weed out whom he did not like in the factory. He prepared a list of people to be transferred to the second factory and submitted the same to the businessman for his approval. The businessman went through the list and approved of it, instantly. He said to head of the first factory:

"I am very happy. You have done a splendid job."

"Thank you, sir," said head of the first factory.

"I forgot to tell you one thing," said the businessman.

"What is it, sir?" said head of the first factory.

"You will head the new factory," said the businessman.

The words came down upon the head like a bolt from the blue. The head never imagined that he could be head of the second factory.

116. TWO TEACHERS

There were two highly qualified tuition teachers in a town. They ran their own private tuition centres independently. They taught the same subject and they were experts in what they taught. But, unfortunately, it so happened that students opting for private tuitions went largely to only one teacher and very few went to the second teacher.

One day, the second teacher met the first teacher in his house and expressed his anguish. He said:

"I am trying my best to teach students that come to me. But very few students are coming to me."

"I know," said the first teacher.

"I fail to understand why I am not able to attract more number of students," said the second teacher.

"There is a reason for it," said the first teacher.

"What is it?" said the second teacher.

"You teach students all that you know. But students don't want what you know. They want what they need to know," said the first teacher.

The second teacher understood where he went wrong and started teaching what the students needed, not what he knew. Students coming to him increased in numbers.

117. LONG WAITING

A young man wanted to act in films directed by a renowned director. He found out where the director resided, went to him and expressed his desire. The director put some questions to know what acting experience the aspirant had, confirmed to himself that the actor knew about nuances of acting and asked him to see him again after one month at a predetermined place. The actor thanked the director, went away and met the director again, at the appointed time and at the predetermined place. The director excused himself with some pretext and asked the young man to see him after another fortnight. The actor met the director exactly after a fortnight. The director appreciated punctuality of the actor and asked him to see him after a few more days. The young man did the same. Whenever the actor met the director, the director asked the young man to see him after some more time and the young man meticulously did the same. Same thing happened again and again and nearly one year passed by. One day, when the young man met the director in his house and went away to meet him after a few days, in some other place as told by the director, wife of the director took pity on the young man and said to her husband:

"You are very unfair to the young man."

"Why?" said the director.

"You are asking the young man to meet you, and, every time he meets you, you are making him go away with disappointment," said wife of the director.

"I know," said the director.

"Why are you troubling him? You are gaining nothing out of troubling him," said wife of the director.

"I am not doing it purposefully. Unfortunately, whenever he comes to see me, I am finding myself very busy and I am not able to do anything for him. I myself am feeling guilty of my action," said the director.

"Poor man! He has been coming to you with lot of hope for the last one year. Please do give him a chance, before his hope in you fades away," said wife of the director.

"I have decided to give him a chance, at the earliest opportunity, for one specific reason," said the director.

"What is the specific reason?" said wife of the director.

"The young man has won my heart. He has highly impressed me with his punctuality. He met me without fail, wherever and whenever I asked him to meet. His long wait will bear fruit very soon," said the director.

Wife of the director felt very happy. The director kept his word. He gave a chance to the young man to act in his film. The young actor acted well, made his debut and, in his very first attempt, made foundation for a great acting career in his life. His long waiting for a chance to act in a film directed by a great director bore fruit at last.

118. THE YOUNG MAN

A league of young enthusiasts set out to mount a mountain, on which there was an ancient temple in a dilapidated condition. They climbed the mountain, by a stepped way paved with rough stones. When they moved up by some distance, they saw a man in his sixties, sitting all alone on a step and looking expectantly at the temple tower up above. One youngster in the league greeted the man and said:

"You are all alone here. What for did you come to this isolated spot?"

"I came here to go up to see the temple," said the man.

"Then why are you not climbing up?" said the enthusiast.

"I am afraid, I cannot do it," said the man.

"Why do you say so?" said the enthusiast.

"I am pretty old. I doubt if my age will permit me to scale up the mountain," said the man.

"Who says you are old. You are young enough to climb up. Take a lead and take us up to the temple," said the enthusiast.

"Can I do it?" said the man.

"You can do it. Come up. Get up and lead us up," said the enthusiast.

The man's face brightened. He got up and started climbing. He did not get tired. He stood first to climb up the mountain and enter the temple.

119. NO DEATH POTION

A man immensely liked the world. He had friends that he could rely on, family members that he took pride in and acquaintances that were ever ready to support him. He was rich, learned and he lacked nothing that he desired. By all counts, he was a happy man.

Suddenly his parents passed away, one after another in a quick succession. The sudden death of his parents saddened him deeply. The man could not adjust to the reality that he had to live without his parents. He thought how great it could be if there was some potion that could make mortals immortal. He went to many doctors for potion for immortality. No doctor had a solution. On the advice of a saint, he went into forest, dwelt for long in a cave and sat in penance for god to appear before him. The god, at last, pleased with sincere prayers of the devotee, appeared before him and said:

"Tell me what do you want from me?"

"I want a potion, by which I can conquer death," said the man.

In a trance, the god held out two pots of potions and gave them to the man. The man looked at the potion pots and said:

"What are these pots?" said the man.

"One pot has potion that can put off death. Second pot has potion that gets instant death," said the god.

"I only want a potion that can make me win over death, not the one that gets me death," said the man.

"Keep both of them with you. The potion that gets you instant death may also be of use to you, at some point of time," said the god.

The devotee left the pot, with potion that brought death, in the cave, consumed the potion that made him immortal and went home. He was very happy. The very thought that he won over death electrified him. He lived on in the company of whom he loved and what he liked for many years. A few generations passed. All those that were dear and near to the man died long ago and went into oblivion. The man remained on earth all alone like a truncated tree. Without the ones with whom he moved, he found it very difficult to live on solitarily. He got vexed with the lifeless life that he lived. He felt all of a sudden that there was no more charm in living. He wanted to die. But he could not do it. He wished how good it could be if death came to him and took him away from loneliness that he suffered from. Suddenly he remembered the death potion that the god gave him. He went to the cave, where he left the death potion, got hold of the pot that dusted in one corner, opened it, consumed the potion and died on the spot.

120. BIRTH OF GOD ON EARTH

A young man, who launched himself into the world after studies, observed that there were many things in the world that he did not like. Wide spread corruption in public life, wrong doings in personal life, selfishness, narrow-mindedness, lawlessness, oppression, suppression, exploitation, inequality, living in falsehood and many other undesirable and despicable elements in society made him very sad. The young man got disenchanted with the world that he lived in. He strongly believed in god. He prayed to god. The god appeared before him and said:

"What has made you call me?"

"I understand that whenever there is immorality rampant in society, you take birth on earth and save the society," said the young man.

"I do it," said the god.

"There is total lawlessness in the society in which I am. What are you still waiting for to take birth on earth and save the society from further downfall?" said the young man.

"I am not waiting," said the god.

"What else are you doing?" said the young man.

"I have already taken birth," said the god.

"Where are you?" said the young man.

"In front of you," said the god.

The young man looked at the god before him. The god was no more there. In place of the god that stood before him until then, there came up a mirror in which the young man saw his own image.

121. REWARD FOR GOOD ACT

A young scholar learnt how to chant Vedas from his learned father. Every day, he sat in assembly hall of an ancient temple that was located on a hillside and rendered the recitation methodically, metrically, musically and mellifluously. The serene environs of the temple, with peepul, banyan and neem trees casting their cool shades on the temple precincts, reverberated with sounds of music, generated out of the recitation. By and large, no devotee visited the temple that was away from human habitation. The scholar was all alone by himself in the tranquil place. He did not recite for anyone. He did it for sheer pleasure that he derived from the recital.

One day, the scholar went through his recitation, all alone in the temple. After he finished the recitation and opened eyes, he saw a traveller seated before him and listening with deep absorption. When the recitation stopped, the traveller opened his eyes, looked at the little scholar with respect and said:

"You have mesmerised me with your recitation."

"I am honoured with your words," said the young scholar.

"Do continue what you are doing. You are carrying forward a great tradition," said the traveller.

"I want to do it. I am doing it. But I do not know, how long I shall continue to do this," said the young scholar, with a tinge of philosophical resignation in his tone.

"Why do you say so?" said the traveller.

"At times, I feel that I shall continue to do this and there will be none to recognise me," said the young scholar.

"Do not get desperate. You are doing a good job. Take my words for granted. A day will come when you will be crowned with recognition," said the traveller.

"I wish your words will come true," said the young scholar.

The traveller went away. The young scholar remained looking on in the direction of going away of the traveller. He cradled in his mind a thought that how good it could be if words of the traveller became true. He continued to live with the practice of rendering the recitation.

After a few weeks, a horse drawn chariot came to the temple from king of the land to take the young scholar to court of the king. The scholar travelled in the chariot to palace of the king. The king praised the scholar, for the command he had on the Vedas, in presence of his courtiers, and rewarded him richly. It took some time for the scholar to realize that the king was no other than the traveller that sat before him in the temple and heard him recite the Vedas.

122. LAYING ROAD

A few forest dwellers lived in a tribal hamlet situated in a dense forest. The dwellers in the hamlet lived far away from a town, where medical and other facilities were available. The dwellers travelled long distances to go to the town for each and everything that they we needed to meet their basic needs. They went on foot, by winding foot tracks, since there was no proper way out of the forest to the town.

Once, the wife of a young tribal youth fell sick. Herbal treatment by a local practitioner of medicine did not yield any result. Health of the sick lady deteriorated, day by day. The local doctor advised the youth to take his wife at once to town for further treatment. The youth could not do it, because there was no proper road leading out of the forest. The youth made his wife sit in a basket, put the basket on his head and went on foot to the nearest town that took for him nearly twelve long hours. Doctor in the town checked up condition of the patient and gave medication. But the medication did not work, since it was too late for the patient to respond to the treatment. The patient died. The youth reached back home with a broken heart.

The youth did not recover from shock of his wife's death for a few weeks. He remained confined to his home. Later on, he recovered and started on a gigantic project. That was to lay a road from his village to the nearest town. When he started the project, everyone in the hamlet dissuaded from doing it, since it was impossible for him to do it. But the youth paid no heed to what others said. He worked on the project continuously and he finished it only by when he turned old. He made a road wide enough for bullock carts to move. Someone asked the man:

"What is it that you have achieved out of laying this road? You have turned old enough to use it."

"I have not laid the road for me. I laid it with a view that it should not be too late for anyone in the village to reach a doctor for medical treatment," said the man.

123. ON A PATH OF RISE

A king wanted to wage war against a neighbouring king. He took opinion of his advisers. Every one of his advisors supported viewpoint of the king. The king ordered for preparations for a war. Before he went on a war, he wanted to take opinion of a saint, in whom he had immense faith. He went to the saint and said:

"I am on my way to wage war against a neighbouring kingdom. Be pleased to bless me with success."

"Drop the idea of war," said the laconic saint, with no further elaboration.

The king took words of the saint as order. He paid respects to the saint, returned to his palace and ordered for dropping of the war move. A few years passed. One day, when the king watched a dance programme in his palace, the saint suddenly dropped into his presence and said:

"Go on war, this instant."

The king was surprised. But he had unflinching faith in the saint. He swung into action. He waged a war against the kingdom, which he wanted to fight a war with, long ago, won the war and annexed the kingdom to his empire. He went to the saint, paid obeisance and said:

"I came to ask for a clarification."

"What is it?" said the saint.

"Last time you advised me against war and this time you advised me for it. Is it because my stars were bad earlier and they are good now?" said the king.

"My advice has nothing to do with your stars," said the saint.

"Then what is the reason for your changed stance on war?" said the king.

"Earlier when you proposed war, your enemy king was on a path of rise. He was on upward trajectory. He was in the process of consolidating his forces and establishing himself as a mighty king. Had you waged war that time, you could have lost the war or suffered heavy losses," said the saint.

"How about this time?" said the king.

"Your enemy king is on a path of fall. He is on a downward trajectory. Defeating him is very easy," said the saint.

The king thanked the saint for his wise advices and returned to his palace.

124. RAVE PARTY

Party culture became a sort of mad craze for some hi-fi students of a college in a town. On every possible occasion, the students went for parties on a big scale. They bunked classes, stole away from campus of the college, went to resorts located in far off places and revelled in rave parities that ran all throughout day and night. They smoked tobacco, took drugs, drank alcohol and revved up in the parties. They talked about politics and ideologies, segregated into groups and differed seriously with one another. Many a time, they brought to fore rivalries that existed within themselves, got into heated arguments and fracas and went to the extent of raining blows on one another.

News of indecent behaviour of the students reached a young police officer in the town. She went to the college, spoke to the Principal and prevailed upon him to counsel the rave party students against the rave parties. The Principal obliged request of the police officer and advised the concerned students. But the good words of the Principal fell on deaf ears of the students. The students that took to rave party culture continued their parties, with no let up in their spirits.

In the wee hours of one night, when a rave party was on in full swing, in a resort situated far away from town, and the revellers exceeded their limits of decency in public life, a police party raided the resort and took the revellers into custody.

By next day, reports of the arrest appeared in the newspapers. The news spread like a wildfire in the town. A lady activist in the town gathered a group of likeminded people, led a procession to the police station, where the arrested students were housed, and demanded for an appointment with the police officer. The police officer did not grant the appointment. The activist was enraged. She addressed a public meeting in front of the police station, condemned action of the police officer and spoke vociferously that the police officer had no right to do moral policing. She received wide applause from the assemblage. When she was on her way to continue a spirited speech on what freedom students had and how their rights of freedom were usurped by law enforcing authorities, a constable from the police station brought a word to the activist that the police officer wanted to see her. The activist felt jubilant with her victory. With no hesitation, she rushed inside the police station and met the lady police officer. The lady officer received the activist with due respect and said:

"I am very sorry for the action that I have taken. I should not have done what I have done."

"It is fine officer. I am happy to note that you have realized your mistake," said the activist.

"Thank you, madam. Take with you your daughter home," said the police officer.

"My daughter!" exclaimed the activist.

"Your daughter is one among those that took part in yesterday's rave party. She is in the cell. Please take her," said the police officer.

The activist, with surprise and shock writ on her face, got up instantly, went inside the cell, saw her daughter there, gave a slap on her cheek, held her hand firmly and brought her out of the cell. The lady police officer got up from her seat and said:

"Madam, be assured that I have not registered any case against your daughter as well as other students arrested yesterday. I would like to vow that, in future, I shall not do any moral policing."

The activist was half dead with shame. She could not stare straight into face of the lady police officer. She remained unmoved for some time and tried to walk out of the police station. But she could not do it. She turned back, went to the police officer and said:

"I am very sorry. Please do not refrain from taking action against revellers in rave parties. Do take action."

The activist, smitten with shame, dragged her daughter calmly out of the police station. The crowd outside the station melted down, in no time.

125. TALE OF TRINITY GODS

People in a town had immense faith in trinity gods. They believed that worshipping Brahma, Vishnu and Siva ritualistically was good for them and their family members. They performed the worship for three, five or seven consecutive days, once or twice in every year, with utmost devotion. Reading a story of the trinity gods was part of the worship.

The wife of a farmer performed the worship, once in every one year, in her house. Since none in her family was literate enough, she depended on someone or other in her street to read tale of the trinity gods in the worship. Many times, she felt how good it could be, if her son, who was not yet literate enough to read the story, became literate enough and read the story for her.

One day, the farmer asked his son to read the tale of trinity gods. The boy took the book in his hands and started reading it. But he could not read it. He dwelt on every word and took a long time to complete one sentence and move to the next sentence. The farmer was dejected. He expressed his displeasure to his son and went away.

Wife of the farmer took a clue from the incident. She made it a practice to sit with her son and make him read the story regularly. The boy read the story very slowly, initially. But over a period of time, he picked up speed and started reading the story fast enough. That her own son read independently the tale of trinity gods thrilled the lady.

When the lady found that her son was in a position to read the story, she organised a weak long worship for trinity gods in her house, invited devotees from other houses in her neighbourhood and made her son read out the story in the worship. The boy faced hiccups initially to read, in presence of other devotees sitting in the worship, but overcame the same very soon. He finished reading the story successfully to satisfaction of all. The farmer's wife felt very happy to realize that her long cherished dream came true and her son read the story in the worship.

The boy, who read the story, was equally thrilled. He was overwhelmed with happiness. He especially liked when other devotees in the worship complimented him for his successful reading. For appreciation from others, the boy practised reading the story again and again in his leisure hours and picked up speed in reading. Over a period of time, he became the fastest reader in the locality. Many householders in the locality, who went for worship of trinity gods, invited the boy to read the story and the boy read it very happily.

The boy continued to read the tale of trinity gods, again and again, in various households. In the process, he developed interest in reading. The interest spilled and spread to study subjects in his school. Eventually, the boy gained foothold in his studies and won laurels.

CONCLUSION

Trillions of people lived on earth before us. They lived their lives the way they liked and the way they could. They took birth, lived on earth and went into oblivion. They showed us how to live life and how not to live it. We needs must study way of life of our predecessors, through history and literature, and arrive at how we should live life and how we should not.

There is nothing like absoluteness in how we can live our life. People that lived yesterday lived lives better than those that lived before them. We in the present are trying to lead lives better those that lived yesterday. The lives that we are living today are going to become benchmarks for those that will come to live tomorrow. Let us live lives in such a way that our future generations will take pride in our way of life.

We can do anything that we want in our life. We can either run after materialistic gains and forget about spiritualistic aspects or run away from life and pursue only spiritualistic gains or strike a right balance between them and lead a wholesome life. We must decide for ourselves what and how we should do it.

Happiness is the bliss of life. We must do only that act that gives us happiness. We can get happiness, if we have limited needs, we respect the principle of co-existence, we live in peace with ourselves and we live in peace with the external world. If we don't do it, we are surely prone to encounter unhappiness. We ought to purchase happiness at any cost and drive away unhappiness, even at a higher cost.

Mother earth is the only planet in the entire universe, known to support life. Life on earth thrives, only if earth is intact. Man for materialization of his unlimited greed and in mad pursuit of material riches has over exploited earth and caused extensive damage to ecological system on earth. It is bounden duty of one and all of us to put a stop to mindless destruction that we have wrought so far to nature and preserve the great earth in the lap of which we are living securely.

Man in the past has committed many mistakes. He fought countless wars that led to extinction of many tribes and races. He suffered heavily from it. He learnt it the hard way that war is not a solution for a problem and it is to be avoided at any cost. Let us keep note of what mistakes the man before us committed and take cue from it not to repeat the mistakes.

Let us live with amity. There is no place for enmity in our lives. Let us live with magnanimity. There is no place for ignominy in our lives. Let us adopt give and take policy. Let us follow live and let live concept in true spirit of it. We are intelligent. We can think and get to know what we ought to do and ought not to do. Let us think. Let us do what is good for us and others. Every living creature on earth has right to live. Let us help support life on earth.

Let the ideas that have found place in tales of this book provide stimulus to readers to introspect. Let us think coolly, adopt what is good and desirable in our way of life, strive to live life better than what we are living at present and become world class citizens.